The Mysterious Misadventures of Clemency Wrigglesworth

The Mysterious Misadventures of Clemency Wrigglesworth

JULIA LEE

OXFORD

UNIVERSITY PRESS

OXFORD
UNIVERSITY PRESS

Great Clarendon Street, Oxford OX2 6DP
Oxford University Press is a department of the University of Oxford.
It furthers the University's objective of excellence in research, scholarship,
and education by publishing worldwide in

Oxford New York

Auckland Cape Town Dar es Salaam Hong Kong Karachi
Kuala Lumpur Madrid Melbourne Mexico City Nairobi
New Delhi Shanghai Taipei Toronto

With offices in

Argentina Austria Brazil Chile Czech Republic France Greece
Guatemala Hungary Italy Japan Poland Portugal Singapore
South Korea Switzerland Thailand Turkey Ukraine Vietnam

Oxford is a registered trade mark of Oxford University Press
in the UK and in certain other countries

British Library Cataloguing in Publication Data

Data available

ISBN: 978-0-19-273367-2

1 3 5 7 9 10 8 6 4 2

Printed in Great Britain

Paper used in the production of this book is a natural,
recyclable product made from wood grown in sustainable forests
The manufacturing process conforms to the environmental
regulations of the country of origin

To B, with thanks for your love and support
and all those cups of—drink of the gods!—tea.

Chapter 1

'Such a quiet little thing'

—++○++—

Clemency Wrigglesworth stood at the foot of the gangway and stared up at the big white ship. England—it was taking her to England. At least she hoped it was, if they would let her on board. She had never been to England before. She had never been on a ship before.

'Hurry up, missie! You can't stand there all day!' The man behind her was puffing and blowing, trying to get past.

Clemency stepped onto the gangway.

At the top, a line of sailors all in white uniforms stood in the blazing mid-morning sun, greeting the passengers as they came on board. The captain, in his peaked cap, waited at the end of the line.

'Good morning, good morning,' he smiled at everyone. He wasn't very tall, but when Clemency reached

1

him he bent his head down to her level. 'Good morning! And who might you be?'

'Clemency Wrigglesworth.'

'You'll have to speak up, young lady. Your voice is very quiet.'

'Clemency Wrigglesworth. I've got a ticket.' In case he didn't believe her, she waved it under his sunburned nose. 'And luggage.' She pointed down at the dock, where three tin boxes and a cabin trunk formed a teetering pile. The name Wrigglesworth was stencilled on the sides in square black letters.

'I'm sure you have,' the captain said. 'And where is your family? Or your friends?'

Clemency bit her lip. 'I'm on my own.'

The captain frowned. 'Are you sure?'

He turned to the purser, who stood beside him with the passenger list, and asked, 'Are we expecting another unaccompanied child?'

The purser ran his finger down the list, shaking his head slowly. It took an agonizingly long time before he came to the Ws. 'Mrs Lucie Wrigglesworth, Miss Clemency Wrigglesworth,' he read out.

'Mrs Lucie Wrigglesworth? Would that be your mother?'

Clemency nodded.

'And is she with you?'

Clemency shook her head.

'I *see*,' said the captain, and rubbed his jaw.

The man directly behind Clemency in the queue began puffing and blowing again. 'How long is this going to take?' he complained.

The captain said something to the purser in a voice too low for anyone to hear, and then took Clemency to one side and leaned down towards her again.

'You are very young to be travelling alone.'

'I'm eleven,' Clemency said, drawing her small frame up as tall and as wide as she could.

'Alone,' the captain went on, 'with no arrangements made for someone to look after you during the voyage. Where is your mother? According to my list, she's expected on board ship.'

'She couldn't come.'

'Is she unwell?'

'She *was* unwell,' Clemency said.

'Then she's better?'

'No. She got worse.'

The captain's tone became very serious, and he furrowed his brow. 'She's too ill to travel?'

'So ill that she died.'

The captain stood up straight again. His face registered shock. 'And have you no other relatives, or friends?'

'No,' said Clemency, in a whisper. 'At least, only in England. That's where we were going when my mother fell ill, so that's where I'm going now. I *must*. I haven't got a home in India any longer. And I *have* got a ticket.' She waved it again, just to prove her point.

He signalled to one of the officers waiting in line. 'Take this young lady to my cabin, and find Mrs Potchard.'

At least I'm on board ship, thought Clemency. At least I've got this far. But she could feel her knees shaking beneath her.

The captain's cabin was dark and stuffy. Clemency sat on a chair and swung her legs. This reminded her of the hotel where, for the past three weeks, she had sat on overstuffed chairs and swung her legs and waited for the ship to arrive in Bombay. One after another, different people had tried to take charge of her. Old ladies with whiskery faces had snapped

4

orders at her. Young ladies with sharp noses asked her endless questions. And gentlemen with big moustaches stared at her and said, 'Well, well!' and never said anything more at all. They were all very interested in her *situation*, but none of them seemed very interested in *her*.

A steward put his head around the cabin door. 'You must be the young lady. Would you like anything to drink while you're waiting?'

Clemency nodded. When he came back with a glass of ice-cold lemonade, she asked, 'Please—what is it that I'm waiting for?'

'They've sent to find Mrs Potchard for you.'

'Mrs Potchard?'

Clemency wondered if she was the person who dealt with problematical children, with would-be stowaways, the person who was in charge of throwing them off the ship or handing them over to the Bombay police.

'Mrs Potchard looks after unaccompanied children on the voyage. If they're going home to England to start school, or when they sail out to India to join their families again, she takes care of them.'

'Oh.'

'She's a very pleasant sort of lady.' And the steward winked.

Usually when grown-ups said someone or something was pleasant, it turned out to be the opposite. Clemency could just imagine what Mrs Potchard would be like. Parents and guardians the length and breadth of the British Empire trusted her to ferry their children about the world. She would be like the strictest governess, and the fussiest nursemaid, and the bossiest old aunt, all rolled into one. Clemency pictured her as very tall and thin, with sharp eyes and a stern expression, and wearing a mud-coloured dress that she never changed.

Suddenly she heard a noise outside in the corridor. She recognized the captain's voice, saying, 'She's a peaky little thing. I damn well hope she isn't ill herself.'

Then a woman's voice replied, 'Half the passengers could be carrying something infectious, you know, Captain. And you're not intending to turn *them* off the ship!'

Clemency stopped swinging her legs and kept perfectly still.

The captain went on, 'If I may speak plainly, she doesn't seem terribly upset by it all.'

'Probably still reeling from the shock,' replied the woman. And suddenly they were both in the room.

The captain made a bow, the sort of half-bow that a short person makes in a narrow space, and said, with a flourish, 'I beg to present—Mrs Potchard!'

Clemency opened her mouth, but nothing came out.

Mrs Potchard was hardly taller than Clemency herself. Her face was plump and cheerful, her cheeks and nose scattered with freckles. Untidy red-gold curls sprang out from under a lace cap. Her round little body, wrapped in a bright Paisley shawl, was shaped just like a barrel.

'I'm so pleased to meet you!' she said, and held out her hand to Clemency. 'I'm on this ship to take the Chope twins off to school in England. I do this all the time, you see. Everyone from the Viceroy down has seen fit to use my services. My terms are most reasonable. Captain Christmas has explained to me about your little—er—predicament.'

She glanced towards the captain, who bowed again, and nodded at her to go on.

'I would be very happy to oversee *your* journey as well, my dear. But only if you would be happy with my company.'

Well, that's new, Clemency thought. Nobody had ever consulted her before, about anything. She ate the food that was dished up, wore the clothes the servants put out for her, read the books her governess told her to, attended other children's parties because she was invited. But no one ever asked her what *she* thought about it all, or what *she* wanted.

Mrs Potchard sat down in the chair opposite. She lowered her voice and leaned across the small gap between them. 'And Captain Christmas is quite anxious that *someone* should look after you. You can share my cabin, rather than be on your own.'

'Will he throw me off the ship if I say no?'

Mrs Potchard's eyes grew very round and wide. 'Oh no! I'm sure he wouldn't do that. Where would you go?'

'Exactly,' said Clemency in a low voice. She leaned even nearer to Mrs Potchard. 'I'd be glad to have your company. Thank you for asking me. But I haven't any money to pay you. Not even on the most *reasonable terms* in the world.'

Mrs Potchard shook her head. 'Never mind. We won't worry about that until we get to England. I'm sure your relatives will be extremely relieved to have you safe home with them. They'll be more than happy to meet my expenses.'

'Yes,' said Clemency, but there was a shiver of doubt in her voice. For she had absolutely no idea who her relatives in England were . . .

'This is the first ship I've ever been on,' Clemency said. They were walking on the deck. Bombay slid away behind them in the hazy distance. 'I was born in India, and I've never left it. Before today.'

'And I've been to sea hundreds of times,' said Mrs Potchard. 'But my charges often haven't. The Chope twins—' and she nodded ahead to where two boys of eight or nine years old scuttled about, 'have never been away before now. They're off to boarding school. I expect at present they're missing their mama and papa.'

'I expect so,' Clemency agreed, stiffly. The twins, as alike as a duck and its reflection, looked incapable of missing anything but their tea.

Mrs Potchard gazed out over the wrinkling blue sea and said slowly, 'I expect you . . . ?'

Clemency knew what she was going to say. She felt disappointed. After such a promising start, Mrs Potchard was going to turn out just like all the people at the hotel. They pretended to be kind, but all they wanted to do was *find out* about her, so that they could go away and gossip to their friends. *'That poor little orphan, do you know what she just told me about her dear sweet mother? Well—'*

'. . . could do with your tea?' Mrs Potchard finished.

'My tea?'

'You must be hungry, child. When did you last eat?'

Clemency tried to think. Lunchtime had passed while she waited to board, and she had been so nervous at breakfast that she hadn't been able to swallow a single mouthful. As she thought about her stomach, a sudden angry growl came out of it.

'I think that speaks for itself,' said Mrs Potchard, and she called out, 'Twins! Come here at once!' And they did.

Over tea, Clemency told Mrs Potchard, quite of her own accord, 'I don't really miss Mama because I hardly ever saw her. I saw my father even less. The thing I loved best about India was Treasure. I miss him. Treasure was a horse,' she explained.

'*Your* horse?'

'Oh, no! He belonged to Colonel Hibbert. But I saw him nearly every day and always took him a sugar lump. He was very big and gentle, and bright shiny chestnut, like a new coin.'

'Did your parents give you a horse of your own?'

'Never.'

'Or a little pony?'

'No. Nothing like that.'

Mrs Potchard gave her a thoughtful look, as if she were taking in a piece of information and storing it up for future use.

'Do you mind if I ask, had you any brothers or sisters?'

Clemency found that she didn't mind—too much—if Mrs Potchard asked.

'No, I was the only one. I had to share my governess with a girl called Phoebe Glover-Smith.'

'Glover-Smith? With brothers called Tom and Arthur?' Mrs Potchard's eyes shone and she laughed as if she was remembering something delicious. 'Naughtiest boys I ever met!'

'Were they?' said Clemency, delighted. 'Mrs Glover-Smith always told me that they were *such* well-mannered children, and *so* devoted to their studies, quite the opposite of Phoebe and me.'

So then they were off on a long conversation about Mrs Potchard's past charges.

'I don't think I've ever talked so much, all at one time,' Clemency told Mrs Potchard. 'Mama always said that I was such a quiet little thing. Timid, too.'

Mrs Potchard fixed her with a sharp look, but there was a distinct gleam in her eye. 'Is that so? In my experience, there is no such thing as a *really* quiet child. As for timid—no, I'm sure you'll discover you are hardly that. If you were timid you would never have got yourself as far as this ship.'

Clemency thought about this. She was quiet because at home that was what it was best to be. When Mama wasn't out at a dance or a party she was lying down, tired out, or complaining of a headache. And she was timid around her father. He was a fierce man with a loud voice and a sudden temper. He didn't want a child under his feet. She shook her head quickly, and tried not to think any more about that.

'You have *inner resources*, my dear,' said Mrs Potchard.

Clemency blushed. She was not accustomed to receiving compliments and didn't know what to do. So she changed the subject.

'Do you enjoy life on the high seas?' she asked.

'I adore travelling. And this ship is the very best in the P&O line, and Captain Christmas is the very best captain. So you've struck lucky here.'

'I've never heard of anyone whose name was *really* Christmas,' Clemency told her.

'Yes, Captain Francis Drake Christmas. He comes from a long line of sailors. But, unlike his namesake, he is very law-abiding. Not one bit piratical.'

Clemency frowned. 'Sir Francis Drake wasn't a *pirate.*'

'Of course he was!' said Mrs Potchard. 'All seafaring folk in those days were pirates first, and patriots after. Where did you learn your history?'

Clemency folded her hands primly and said, 'From Palmer's *History of The World for Children (In Three Parts)*, of course.'

'Of course,' echoed Mrs Potchard. 'Mr Palmer clearly left out the most interesting parts.'

Mrs Potchard's cabin was modest, but shipshape and very tidy. Clemency's luggage had been delivered and took up rather a lot of the room between the narrow beds. Clemency had just put on her nightgown and was brushing her hair when Mrs Potchard came in and sat down on the edge of her own bunk.

'We really need to find out who your relatives are in England,' she announced. 'Are you sure you know nothing about them?'

Clemency shook her head. 'No. Nothing at all.'

'If you don't mind, I'll go through your belongings. There must be a clue of some sort. After all, if there isn't, what will I do with you once we reach Southampton?' Mrs Potchard sounded cheerful enough, but Clemency felt bleak. 'I'm sure we can find out. The sooner we start, the sooner we'll have something.'

Mrs Potchard opened the smallest tin box. It contained only Clemency's clothes, her meagre store of toys and books. Next they worked through the bigger boxes, which were filled with her mother's belongings: dresses, shoes, underwear. At last Mrs Potchard sat back on her heels and exclaimed, 'This looks promising!'

She held up a small packet of letters, tied with a black ribbon.

'Do you mind if I take a look?'

Clemency shook her head.

Mrs Potchard unfolded the letters and quickly glanced through them. She scarcely seemed to have time to read one before she went on to the next.

'These appear to be letters from your father to your mother when he was away with the regiment,' she said, 'And these are from friends on hearing of his death.' She paused. 'Aha! What have we here?'

At the bottom of the pile were two very old and creased letters. Clemency could see how dirty and yellowed the paper had become.

'Hmm,' said Mrs Potchard. 'These are addressed from the Great Hall, Caredew, near Frome, Somerset.' She frowned and peered more closely. 'One is signed with the initials H.T.L. And the other—in humbler writing, to my mind, it has many crossings-out and misspelt words—is signed simply from "Molly".'

Mrs Potchard read the contents of the letters to herself, with a certain amount of gentle head-shaking. But all she said to Clemency was, 'Good. Now we have an address in England, if not a name. We can put an advertisement in *The Times,* asking for someone to come and fetch you. I'm sure it will be quite straightforward.'

She gave Clemency a bright, confident smile. But Clemency didn't smile back.

Chapter 2
Gully

━━━━◦━━━━

Clemency had never seen so many white faces—and dull brown clothes—as she found waiting for them on the quay at Southampton. The air was full of smoke and fine clinging rain, and so cold! She thought she would much rather stay on board and sail straight back to the sunshine. However, Mrs Potchard got them swiftly disembarked. She was organizing a porter to carry the luggage when a gangly youth came up behind her and grabbed her by the waist.

'What the—?' she shrieked, whisking round. Her face broke into the broadest of smiles. 'Gully, you wicked beast! Give your mother a kiss!'

They hugged enthusiastically. Clemency stood to one side, feeling awkward, while the Chope twins took the opportunity to start a wrestling match.

It hadn't occurred to Clemency that Mrs Potchard would have any sons or daughters of her own. After all, what would they do with themselves while she was sailing all over the world, looking after other people's children? Gully Potchard was about fourteen or fifteen. He had his mother's freckles, and her springy red curls, but he was immensely tall and thin, and wearing a coat and trousers that looked as if he had recently outgrown them.

After she had enquired about his health and his diet, Mrs Potchard introduced her charges to him. 'These are the Chopes. Stand still, twins, and straighten your collars.' They did so at once. 'And this is Miss Clemency Wrigglesworth. Miss Wrigglesworth is a mystery, and I have some instructions for you in connection with her. But first, you can find us a cab.'

'Got one waiting, Ma,' Gully said, in a voice which fluted interestingly up and down.

'But we'll need *two*. One to take the twins and myself to the station, and another to drop you and Miss Wrigglesworth at Wentworth Gardens.'

She handed Gully an envelope.

'This is the wording of an advertisement you are to place in *The Times*, calling for Miss Wrigglesworth's relations to make themselves known. She can board with Hetty until they come to fetch her. I shall be back in a day or two.'

Mrs Potchard leaned forward, and for a moment Clemency thought she was going to kiss her goodbye, but she just brushed a lock of rain-damp hair from Clemency's forehead. Then she jumped into the cab and waved the driver to whip up his horse.

Was I just another assignment? Clemency wondered. Just one more child amongst the hundreds of children who passed through her hands?

She climbed slowly up into the second cab. It smelled of mouldy cushions. She leaned back and closed her eyes, letting Mrs Potchard's words float in her head. *Wentworth Gardens*: it sounded such a lovely *English* place. Back in India, everyone talked of England with such longing. She imagined Wentworth Gardens to be just like the pictures she had seen in books; lush green lawns surrounded by beds overflowing with beautiful flowers. And in the middle, perhaps, a magnificent fountain spraying water into a basin shaped like a giant shell. It would be a relief to get to Wentworth Gardens.

The cab bumped noisily over a pothole and Clemency jerked awake. She wiped the mist off the cab window, and peered out to see if she could spot the gardens. But there was nothing outside except close grey walls, streaked with wet. Rows of dirty windows, and mean front doors. They must still have a long way to go.

Abruptly the cab stopped. Gully flung open the door and leapt out. The cabman set her boxes down in the road, and then clattered off again into the smog.

Clemency found herself alone with Gully Potchard at the end of a narrow, rain-sluiced alley of terraced houses. Each had a door that led straight off the street, with only three worn stone steps between it and the pavement. There wasn't a flower or a single blade of grass in sight, certainly not a fountain. No garden of any sort.

'Hey, you!' Gully shouted at a small boy, dressed in filthy hand-me-downs, who was hopping in and out of the gutter-water. 'Here's a farthing. Mind those boxes for me till I gets someone as can fetch 'em.' His voice was different now, rougher than when he had spoken to his mother.

The boy caught the coin that Gully threw him with one quick hand, grabbing it out of the air. He went on hopping, but kept a determined eye on the luggage.

'This way.' Gully jerked his head at Clemency. He was no longer polite. 'Wrigglesworth, eh? That's a funny name.'

Clemency surprised herself by retorting sharply, 'So's Potchard, for that matter.'

Gully grinned. 'So it is. A pochard's a duck. Did you know that? Not spelt the same, but sounds it. A little diving duck with a bright-red head. Would you believe it?' And he rubbed at his own red hair.

'Here we are. Number seventeen.'

He pointed at a particularly depressing house. Instead of approaching the front door, he leaned over the railing which overlooked a tiny basement area, and shouted, 'Less-STAH!' in a voice fit for a sergeant-major.

A window below flew open with a bang, and a female voice screamed back, 'Oo wants 'im?,' and then, in a different tone, 'Oh, it's *you.*'

Then a short, muscular boy shot out of the basement door. He tripped on the bottom step of the stairs, and climbed the rest in a series of bumps and stumbles.

'Leicester, my good man,' said Gully, clapping a firm hand on his shoulder. 'Fetch your cart. This young lady's a guest and she's got some luggage wants attending to.'

Leicester immediately dived back down the steps, getting there safely more by luck than by judgement.

'Shall we go in?' Gully said to Clemency, in a regal tone. Now he pushed open the battered front door, and made a low bow. Clemency felt sure he was teasing her, but she went in all the same. What choice did she have?

He showed her into the tiny front parlour. The bay window was festooned with layers of grubby lace, which blocked most of the light. A large fern that stood in the centre of the window shut out the rest. The grate was set with coals and kindling, but no fire was lit. It felt hardly any warmer than out in the street.

'You'd like some tea, I expect,' Gully said, pulling the envelope his mother had given him out of his coat pocket as he spoke. 'Ladies usually do. Even *mystery* ladies! Make yourself at home.' And he disappeared.

At home? Clemency shivered miserably and perched herself on a hard chair. Her stomach felt tight with apprehension.

Gully obviously wanted to read the note from his mother—her instructions—in private. Until this last hour, she had felt complete faith in Mrs Potchard, but now she wondered what on earth was going on. To be brought to this grimy street, and this awful house! Gully seemed to change character from one minute to the next. And that rough boy, Leicester, and the screaming female downstairs? Not at all the sort of people she expected to be associated with the well-mannered, reliable Mrs Potchard, who was, after all, trusted by the Viceroy himself!

What was really in that letter of instruction? Was she directing him to send a ransom note rather than placing an enquiry in *The Times*? Clemency decided that England—far from paradise—was a dismal, frightening place.

Her anxious thoughts were interrupted by bumping and banging outside. She went to the window and peered out. Leicester was unloading her luggage from a cart made of scrap wood and what looked like parts of an old baby-carriage. He hauled the biggest trunk up the steps and stood it on end to fit it through the front door. It crashed to the floor, shaking the whole house.

'Less-STAH!' shrieked the banshee from downstairs. A thudding up the inside staircase, and the shrill voice came nearer. 'What the jinks is going on up there? Half my pies is on the floor—jumped clear off the pastry board!'

Next came Gully, hard on her heels. 'Just shifting the young lady's luggage, Aunt Hett. You bring a lot of stuff when you're coming back from India for good an' all.'

Then all three—Leicester, Gully, and the owner of the banshee voice—crammed themselves into the parlour doorway to peer at Clemency. She felt like a creature in a zoo.

Gully said, 'I'd better introduce—my aunt Hetty Marvel, my cousin Leicester—this is Miss Clemency Wrigglesworth, late of India, soon to be of the Great Hall, Caredew, near Frome.' Waving his letter, he whirled one ridiculously long arm in Clemency's direction. 'As soon as your relations shake out tomorrow's copy of *The Times* they'll be winging their way down here to fetch you. In the meantime, good Aunt Hett has her best room ready for you'—a glance at Hetty, who looked extremely put out—'and there's some fresh-brewed tea right on its way.'

He shuffled them out of the doorway again, saying in a lowered voice, 'Tea, Hett, tea! Never mind your pies. The cat will have had 'em by now.'

Clemency felt her stomach unclench a little. At least Gully appeared to be keeping Mrs Potchard's promise. Perhaps he wasn't so bad, after all. Now he came back in, rubbing his hands together, and bent towards the grate. 'Let's get this old fire a-blazing.'

Tea was eventually brought, with thick toast and blackberry jam. Clemency was surprised at how good it tasted, and the first slice was gone in a moment.

Hetty had taken off her smeared apron, but her hair was still falling in cobwebby strands to her shoulders, and she had a smudge of flour on her nose. She said, with a touch of irritation, 'I can't show you to your room yet, Miss, as Leicester's blocked the first-floor landing with one of your boxes and we're waiting for him to come back with a rope. It's leek pie for supper—I take it you're agreeable to that?'

Clemency could do nothing but nod. She wondered if her pie would be one that had escaped both the floor and the cat.

Chapter 3

Announcing the Arrival . . .

—||—○—||—

The next morning Clemency found breakfast for one set at the table in the front parlour. Gully stood by the fireplace, apparently waiting for her, so she asked him, 'If this is Wentworth Gardens, where are the *gardens*?'

Leicester, who was just coming in with the coal scuttle, laughed. 'Out the back,' he said.

'That's just a yard.'

Clemency had just seen it from the landing window—a mean little square of cracked paving, crisscrossed by washing lines.

'If there ever *were* any gardens,' Gully told her, 'they're beneath the paving stones now.'

Clemency stared gloomily at her breakfast. Even the porridge was grey.

'Cheer up, though. Look at this.' Gully produced a slip of paper which he waved across the table at her.

'What is it?'

'Your advertisement. Didn't Ma say we'd put it in *The Times* for you? Well, here it is, and I even clipped it out so's you could keep it.'

Clemency read the clipping, slowly, so that she could take in every single word. It said:

Announcing the arrival, from India, of Miss C. Wrigglesworth, only daughter of the late Captain Wrigglesworth, and of the late Mrs Lucie Wrigglesworth, formerly of the Great Hall, Caredew, nr. Frome, Somerset. Miss Wrigglesworth awaits at 17 Wentworth Gardens, Southampton.

She frowned. 'It doesn't explain much, does it?'

'There isn't much to explain. It's all that anyone knows.'

Miss Wrigglesworth awaits, Clemency thought, and let out a huge sigh. 'I do hope they won't be long,' she said.

The dirty rain slid down the dirty windows without stopping. Clemency sat in the parlour reading a book she had read twice before, not knowing what else to do. The mantelpiece clock ticked slowly and noisily, but the rest of the house was quiet. She wondered what the other inhabitants were up to, but didn't dare go to find out.

Suddenly the door handle rattled, and a girl bounced into the room. She looked older than Gully, and her hair was done up in a topknot through which she had stuck two knitting needles. Her dress was of spotted yellow silk and over it she wore a tight scarlet jacket. She carried a pair of high-heeled shoes with black ribbons dangling from them.

'I'm Whitby,' she said abruptly. 'How d'you do?'

She had the same pointed features as Hetty but the vivid remains of theatrical make-up were plastered on her face, making her eyes bigger and her mouth more fierce.

'Yes, Whitby bloomin' Marvel. You may have heard of me. And *you* must be Miss C. Wrigglesworth, late of *The Times* personal columns.'

'Yes,' said Clemency, holding out her hand and feeling rather weak.

'What's the C stand for?'

'Clemency,' Clemency whispered.

'Blimey! Almost as bad as mine.' The girl took one of the knitting needles out of her hair and scratched her head with it. 'Don't mind me, I know I look a scare. I've been dancing the matinee show at the Hippodrome, see, and just had time to nip home for a bite of Ma's bread pudding. That makes a girl light on her feet, I can tell you!' And she let out a raucous laugh. 'How old are you, Clemency?'

'Eleven,' answered Clemency, shocked into obedience.

The rest of the family, although clearly bursting with curiosity, hadn't pressed her with questions. Whitby had no time for delicacy. Standing only inches away from Clemency, she opened her wide red mouth and bawled, 'Less-STAH!'

Leicester came rushing up from the kitchen.

'Got a little job for you, darling Bro,' said Whitby. 'My left heel is hangin' half off. Give it a tap with your hammer, could you?'

And Leicester ran eagerly away, the ribbons from the dancing shoes fluttering in his wake.

Whitby pointed at Clemency's pink muslin sleeve, which poked out from under her blue muslin sleeve. 'Is that a petticoat, or what?'

'It's just my dress,' said Clemency, ashamed. 'I put one on top of another. I haven't any warm clothes, you see. I've always lived in India, until now. It's very hot—in India.'

'Never!' said Whitby in a hushed voice, her black-ringed eyes widening. '*Hot?* In *India?* You do surprise me!'

And then she giggled, and Clemency felt even more embarrassed.

'Why don't you get yourself some decent clothes, then?' Whitby went on. ''Stead of lookin' like a scare-crow, and freezin' with it?'

'I'm waiting for my English relations to fetch me. I expect they'll see to all that.' She didn't want to have to tell this girl that she hadn't a single English sixpence to her name.

'Nice for some,' said Whitby. And she flounced out, adding, 'Try not to bring down the *tone* of the place while you're waiting.'

A moment later there came a loud shriek, followed by Whitby shouting, 'Leicester! My heel's come right off! You've ruined it, you clumsy oaf!' She heard Whitby run down the hallway, half-shrieking, half-sobbing, 'Couldn't trust that boy to saw 'is own leg off!' And the front door slammed shut behind her.

Clemency felt an unfamiliar sensation bubble up in her throat: it was laughter.

'Gulli-VAH, come here, will you!?' Hetty screeched. 'Take Miss Wrigglesworth for a stroll round the neigh-bourhood. She could do with the air.'

It was the following morning, and the rain had eased to a fine dreary drizzle.

'*She* could do with the room,' Gully whispered to Clemency as he ushered her into the street. 'Her usual lodgers are out all day, not under her feet. And she wants to clean the parlour.'

'In India, we had servants to do that sort of thing,' Clemency told him.

Gully pulled a face. 'You're not in India now.'

I know, Clemency thought, and shivered inside her thin jacket.

They came to the end of Wentworth Gardens and stopped. On the corner, a pair of scruffy boys were teasing a dog, while a man leaned against the wall, idly watching. Gully looked up and down in both directions.

'We can walk in the park, if you like? It's not far.'

'I thought it would be *green*,' Clemency said, when they got there. She stood under Gully's big black umbrella and stared at the leafless trees, the muddy grass. The air smelled rank, of wet and earth and rot, but not the rich sort of wet and earth and rot she was used to.

'Hmm, November's not the *best* time to see England,' Gully said. 'D'you think you'll take to living here?'

'It depends on what my family is like, I suppose.'

Clemency drew the advertisement out of her pocket. She had read it so many times that she knew the words by heart. Thinking of her time on board ship with Mrs Potchard, she said, 'I hope they'll be kind. And interesting. And good fun.'

She hardly dared hope anything at all, since every time she had pictured something lately, it had turned out to be quite the opposite.

Gully shrugged. 'There's nothing much you can do about families. Take mine—they're all a bit mad, in a way. They have the travelling itch.'

'What's that?' Clemency imagined some horrible skin disease.

'They love to travel. They can't stay still. If they stay put in one place too long, it works on them terribly and they're driven mad with the need to move on. My mother's been round the world more times than a great explorer. And why d'you think Leicester's called Leicester?'

'I've no idea.'

'Because that's where he was born, of course. Aunt Hett and Uncle Bray had a travelling magic show. Hett named the children after the towns they were born in. Only Whitby and Leicester are left at home now, but she's got seven altogether.'

'Seven! And does she still travel about?'

'Not since Uncle Bray died. You can't carry on with half an act. He was the one who did the sawing in half, you see. Hetty was just sawn. That's why she's so—so *umptious*, now. She's used to bright lights and moving about. Now she's stuck here in Southampton running lodgings to make ends meet.'

'Do you think she'll move on, then?'

Gully considered this for a moment. 'Maybe. Maybe not. She wasn't born to it, you see, she just married into it. It's the Potchard side you want to watch. They're the real travellers.'

'So Hetty's not Mrs Potchard's—your mother's—sister?'

'Lord, no. She married my uncle. They changed their name to Marvel when they started touring with the magic show.'

'But if your mama is *Mrs* Potchard, then she must have married into it, too. And so she can't have the real Potchard travelling itch, either, can she?'

Gully grinned hugely. 'Oh, but she has. Ma married her own first cousin—my poor departed pa, Jonas Potchard.' He spun the umbrella over their heads and sent all the silver drops of rainwater flying. 'So I must have a double-strong case of the travelling itch.'

Clemency laughed. 'Heavens! What a complicated family. I hope mine isn't as bad as that.'

When they arrived at the park gates once more, Gully lowered the umbrella so that their faces were hidden beneath its canopy. He narrowed his eyes and asked, 'By the by, did you spot anything unusual after we left Wentworth Gardens?'

'Unusual?'

'There was this man,' Gully went on, 'with bandy legs. Funniest thing, but I got the impression he was following us. Just take a quick squint.'

He half-raised the umbrella again. Clemency peeped

out. There was no one in sight, just empty grass and bare trees. A single pigeon pecked at the mud.

'I can't see anyone.'

Gully shook his head. 'Ah, well.'

They walked through the big iron gates and out on to the main road. Clemency's neck prickled. She glanced round one more time. A black shape flitted between the trees, then slipped out of sight. She hesitated. 'There *was* someone just then.'

'Short fellow? Bandy legs?'

'Tall and thin, in a long coat.'

Gully frowned. 'My mistake. Must be seeing things. Just forget what I said.'

They walked back in silence but, despite Gully's words, neither could get the idea out of their heads.

Chapter 4
A Visitor

————○————

The parlour door opened with a blast of cold air and Mrs Potchard put her head around it. She looked surprised.

'Clemency! I didn't expect to find you still here. No response to the advertisement, yet, my dear?'

Clemency said nothing, just shook her head.

Mrs Potchard pulled off her gloves and unbuttoned her coat. She didn't appear to be worried.

'Perhaps they didn't see the paper. Perhaps the cat was sitting on that bit of it, or—.' She tried to picture the sort of activities that went on at the Great Hall, Caredew. 'Perhaps the butler, when ironing the newspaper nice and flat, got distracted for a moment and let the iron singe that page.'

'Perhaps they don't want anything to do with me.'

Mrs Potchard was brisk. 'Nonsense, child. Of course they will. But we might try advertising again.'

She looked hard at Clemency. The girl was kneeling on the hearthrug, as close to the fire as she could possibly get.

'You need a warm winter outfit—and perhaps you shouldn't turn up at the Great Hall in those things you're wearing now.'

Clemency glanced down at her crumpled skirts. 'I know I look a fright. But I can't afford new clothes.'

'Let's think, my dear. There must be something amongst your mother's things that could be sold. I know it's sad, but I fear it must be done. We could get you a coat and hat, and material for a decent dress. Hetty will help. She's more accustomed to sequins and feathers, but she can sew a good straight seam if she puts her mind to it. I'll ask her this evening.'

Just then Gully appeared, bearing a tray with teapot, cups, and a plate piled high with crumpets.

'Thought we'd toast these up here, since the fire's lit.' He turned to Clemency. 'Ever used a toasting fork? Or did you have servants to do that for you?'

She wasn't sure if he was being mean, but then he winked. Passing her a long-handled fork, he showed her how to spear a crumpet on the end and hold it over the hottest part of the fire.

Mrs Potchard poured the tea, talking all the while. 'We were just discussing Clemency's relatives. I'm sure they will be in touch very soon. If not, I think I should write directly to the Great Hall.'

'We don't know who it is that lives there,' Clemency said.

'True. But we could write to the Master at that address, and that should get to the right person.'

'Can't we just take her there?' asked Gully. 'Like you took the Chopes to their school?'

'Two minor difficulties, Gully, my dear,' said his mother. She raised an eyebrow at him. 'One concerns time, and the other concerns money.'

'Ah,' said Gully, and stared into the fire.

'I have to be at Paddington Station tomorrow to meet the two Topping girls. We stay the night at Dover and take the early ferry to France.'

Clemency looked puzzled. 'Then you don't always travel back and forth to India?'

'Goodness, no! I'd never see my family at all if I did that. But sometimes the short journeys are more bother than the long ones.'

'You'll enjoy the ferry, Ma, if the sea's not too rough. You know you will,' said Gully.

'And then there's the question of finances,' Mrs Potchard went on, determined not to be sidetracked. 'I've had my fee for the twins, but of course I was hoping for something from Clemency's family by now. The Chopes's money has gone to defray a few expenses here.' She paused and gave Gully a deep look. 'So I've nothing in the kitty until I get back from France. What about you?'

Gully shook his head.

'Broke again?' asked his mother.

'Stony,' he replied.

'Then nobody's going anywhere at the moment. Except me, down to the kitchen to refill this teapot.'

When Mrs Potchard had gone, Clemency asked, 'How do you earn your living, Gully?'

'At present I'm engaged in minding a Miss Wrigglesworth, who will turn out to be an heiress and reward me greatly,' he said, smiling.

'What do you do when you're not looking after heiresses?'

'This and that. Whatever I can get. Mostly I find things. Things that have got into unusual places.'

And he reached up behind her ear and removed a green felt pin-cushion, which usually lived on the mantelpiece. Clemency touched her ear. The pin-cushion had certainly not been there before. 'How did you do that?'

'Uncle Bray taught me.' And from behind his own ear Gully produced Mrs Potchard's spectacles, which had last been seen hanging from a chain at her waist. 'And I find things that have gone missing. People pay me to find things for them.'

'What kind of things?'

'Oh, the usual. Watches, rings, keys. I think about them and sometimes I find them.'

Clemency was amazed. 'Why should they pay you to find them? If they thought about the things themselves, they'd be likely to remember where they put them, and find them straight away. At no expense!'

'No—things they have really lost and never would find on their own. I think about the lost thing and sometimes I can see where it is in my mind, and so I go to the place and I find it.'

'Extraordinary,' said Clemency. 'I've never heard of that before. I suppose that *is* worth paying for. How do you find them in your mind?'

'I don't really know. I do best if I can use something linked to the lost thing. For instance, if it's a dog I'm looking for, I'll hold its lead, or its smelly old rug, while I'm trying to conjure it up.'

'I wish you could find my family for me,' Clemency said.

Gully grinned. 'Maybe I will.'

Mrs Potchard went off before breakfast to catch the early train. She left a letter to be posted to the Master at the Great Hall, Caredew, if there was no response to the second advertisement in *The Times*. She propped it up on the parlour mantelpiece, next to the clock.

'Don't forget it's there,' she instructed Gully. 'You're the only sensible one round here. I'm relying on you.'

She gave him a hug, then stepped back. 'What is it? I know you, Gully Potchard.'

'I—it may be nothing, Ma,' said Gully.

'But it may be something. Spit it out.'

'Just, when you leave the house, keep an eye out for a short, bandy-legged man.'

'Why on earth——?'

'Or a tall, thin man in a long coat.'

'Make up your mind. Which is it?'

'Well, there might be two of 'em. I thought yester-day someone was keeping a watch on this street, this house. And then that someone was following me and Clemency. But I couldn't be sure.'

'What would they be doing that for?'

'Haven't a clue, Ma. But you must admit it's odd.'

Mrs Potchard frowned, though she kept her thoughts to herself. She simply hugged Gully again, harder this time, and added, 'Take good care.'

Leicester was sitting on the basement steps, making repairs to his cart, when a pair of well-polished lady's boots appeared on the pavement at the same level as his nose. The boots halted. Their toes turned to face the house. Leicester scrambled to his feet.

'Can I help you?'

A surprised face down looked down at his. 'Is this Wentworth Gardens?'

'Oh, yes.'

The voice sounded suspicious. 'Number seventeen?'

'Certainly is.'

Abandoning his cart, Leicester hauled himself up to pavement level. Hetty had taught him never to neglect business, and this lady looked like business. She was short and broad, wearing a box-shaped grey coat and carrying an efficient handbag. In one gloved hand she held a scrap of paper, which she quickly slipped away inside her bag.

'Who lives here?' she asked.

Leicester puffed out his chest. 'I do. And my ma and my sister. But they're not in this afternoon.'

'And may I enquire your name?'

Leicester puffed some more. He wished he had his cap on so that he could remove it. 'Leicester Marvel, *Hesquire*, at your service. Is it lodgings you're after?'

The lady looked even more surprised. 'Lodgings?'

'Seventeen Wentworth Gardens, theatrical and commercial lodgings,' he told her. He leapt up the steps to the front door and placed one grubby paw on the handle. 'I can show you round, if you like.'

'Lodgings—ah, yes. Yes—I would like to come inside, if I may.'

She followed him, stepping carefully and holding her handbag in front of her like a shield. Beneath her fierce gaze even Leicester could tell the hall looked uninviting, with its faded wallpaper and crooked pictures. An inescapable smell of drains and last night's onions crept up from the basement.

'Er—do you have many guests at present?'

Hetty had also taught Leicester never to admit to an enquirer that business was bad. So he gave a careless shrug and said, 'Mustn't grumble. Always got people passing through. Commercial travellers, people coming and going to the ships.'

'The ships . . .?'

'Oh, not sailors—never them!' Hetty had warned him not to make it sound like a den for drunken sailors. 'Passengers. Passengers with the Peninsular and Oriental Company.'

'Ah, the P&O. Did you say your *other guests* had come from far away?'

Leicester had said nothing of the sort and he wasn't going to be put off from his sales pitch. He took a deep breath and went on, 'And we're very popular with stage folk. Quality acts playing the theatre and the music halls, they make regular stops with us. Would you be in that line of business yourself, Miss—er—Mrs . . .?'

He looked his visitor up and down. There was nothing theatrical about her appearance, no flash of vivid satin, or pencilled-on beauty spot. Her neat coat and modest hat reminded him more of a Sunday School teacher, not that he had much personal experience of them.

'My name's—um—Lysander. Miss Lysander. Yes,' she said, as if making up her mind. 'You were going to show me round.'

'Yes, indeed.' Leicester flung open the door to the front room. The fire had gone out and the air felt distinctly damp and chilly. He flourished an arm about. 'The guests' parlour. All home comforts. Meals served at table.'

Miss Lysander ignored him. Over the mantelpiece there was a mirror. She walked straight across to it, studied her reflection, and began adjusting her hat.

Leicester felt his business opportunity slipping away. He smoothed the tablecloth with nervous hands and shifted the potted fern a bit to the left, then back again. He glanced out of the window, hoping to see his mother or Whitby coming home. The street was empty.

He tried, 'We can offer very reasonable terms, single nights or weekly, depending. How many nights was it you wanted?'

'I shall have to see the bedrooms first.'

'What—*all* of 'em?'

'All of them.'

Miss Lysander met Leicester's eyes in the mirror. She gave him a quizzical look and then seemed to gather her breath. 'I—I represent an orchestra. Yes, a ladies' orchestra, most respectable, a touring ensemble of lady musicians. We shall require a number of rooms.'

She finished at the mirror by patting her lips with a handkerchief and snapping the clasp of her handbag shut. Then she marched to the door. Leicester scurried to get past her and hold it open.

'I'm afraid I can't show you the first floor front. That's already occupied. But we've very pleasant rooms at the . . .'

He was turning towards the ground-floor back bedroom, but Miss Lysander had already begun to climb the stairs and Leicester had to dash after her. He caught up with her on the landing and tried to steer her in the right direction. 'I think you'll find . . .'

But Miss Lysander ignored him. She turned to the front of the house and grasped the door knob of Clemency's room.

'You can't go in there, that's Miss Cl—'

'Whose room did you say it was?' Miss Lysander asked. But without waiting for an answer she gave the door a firm shove.

Leicester shrugged unhappily. 'I suppose—she *is* out at the mo— I dare say it's all right . . .'

'Aha!' Miss Lysander strode into the room, and, finding it empty, stopped dead. She glared around, not like someone inspecting a room for her own use but as if she was grilling it for clues. Then she seized a small dress that was draped over the end of the bed, held it up, and shook it so fiercely that Leicester thought all the buttons would come off.

Chapter 5
Thinking Like Detectives

━┼━○━┼━

'That fool boy, Leicester—what do you think he's done?'

Hetty stood in the hallway, wringing her hands. Unwinding his long scarf, Gully said cheerfully, 'No idea, Auntie, until you tell us.'

He and Clemency had just been for another walk, but this time spotted nothing suspicious.

'A lady called, seeking rooms, and only our Leicester was at home. But he must've put her right off, because she took one look at the rooms, turned on her heel and left! And you know how hard times is in Wentworth Gardens right now.' Hetty's voice rose to a wail. 'I'll bet she went straight to Mrs Hendry's and engaged rooms there instead. Oh, it's a disaster!'

'Where's Leicester now?'

'Downstairs, sulking. You must talk to him, Gully. I can't get no sense out of the boy.'

Clemency stood where she was, uncertain what to do. But Gully gestured that she should go too, so she followed them down to the basement.

The kitchen was dark, and smelled of food and wet wool and singeing fur. An enormous black cat sat with its paws folded on top of the cooking range. Stockings and socks hung steaming on a line above, and a stewpot simmered beside the cat. The table, which took up most of the middle of the room, was covered with any number of things: knitting, combs, teacups, conkers on strings, a glue-pot, a scrapbook, a jam jar with a glass eye staring out of it, and a raw pig's heart in a white enamel basin. There wasn't an inch of space between them.

'Oh, do sit down, Miss Clem,' said Hetty, ushering her to a chair and sweeping some crumbs off it. Clemency sat down, trying not to catch the gaze of the glass eye.

Returning to the topic of their visitor, Hetty demanded, 'Now, Leicester, think! Did she say where she come from? Was it the Victoria Theatre? We might still have a chance if you nipped down there sharpish.'

'She didn't say . . .' Leicester whined, thoroughly miserable.

'Might be at the Hippodrome,' Hetty muttered, almost to herself, 'with that troupe that claims they're genuine Red Indians.'

'Didn't look like a Red Indian to me,' Leicester mumbled, stirring the brush round and round in the glue-pot, splashing flour-and-water paste over the tablecloth and the pig's heart. 'Just a *nordinary* lady.'

'Well, she wouldn't, would she, out of costume?' his mother said, exasperated. She began to pace up and down the floor.

Gully clutched his head. 'Oh, if only Whitby had been here! Then we'd get a rundown from her hat to her boots, with her life history thrown in for good measure.'

'If only Whitby had been here,' Hetty said, 'the lady in question would be settled in the back bedroom by now, and you could see her for yourself.'

Leicester lifted the brush from the glue-pot and began decorating the pig's heart with a series of dots and dashes. 'How many ladies in a ladies' orchestra, d'you think?' he asked.

Hetty stopped pacing. 'A what?'

'I remember now . . . all your shoutin' put me off before. She was after rooms for a ladies' orchestra, and said they was most respectable.'

Hetty shut her eyes and let out a moan of anguish. When she opened them again she noticed what he was doing, and grabbed the brush from him. 'Less-STAH! That's your supper you're painting all over!'

'She didn't look like theatre folk at all,' Leicester insisted. 'First she wanted to see all the rooms, but then when she looked in Miss Clem's room, it was like she'd had enough, and she just took off.'

'Looked in *Clemency's* room?' asked Gully. 'What for?'

Leicester twisted round to glare at him. 'I couldn't stop her. I told her it was occupied, but she just barged in like she'd catch someone up to sumpfing.' Then he turned to Clemency. 'Sorry, Miss. She might have messed up your stuff a bit.'

'What!?' said Gully.

Leicester's voice took on an anguished tone. 'She was one of them nosy, pushy sorts. You know, askin' about who lived here, and who else was stayin' and where they come from. I didn't tell her—well, not much.'

'I hope you didn't tell her we're desperate for custom,' his mother said darkly. 'That's enough to send them on their way.'

Gully looked thoughtful. He leaned towards his cousin and asked him gently, 'Did she give a name?'

'She *did*. But I can't remember it.'

'And did you see anyone in the street when she left— a man, or two men?'

'Too many questions!' Leicester wrapped his arms around his head and laid it on the tabletop. 'Lies . . . lies . . .' he murmured. Suddenly he popped his head up again, cheeks berry-red. 'Lysander! That was 'er name. Lysander. And she had a wart on 'er nose!'

Clemency felt sorry for him. All this fuss because he had let a possible lodger go. But she noticed that Gully had his worried expression back, the one he'd worn the day before, outside the park gates. He got up from the table and signalled to her.

'Let's take a look at your room.'

They left Hetty and Leicester in the stuffy kitchen and climbed the two flights of rickety stairs. Clemency's bedroom door was half-open. She couldn't see any disturbance: the bed was made and her trunks stood where she'd left them beneath the window, their lids firmly shut. The only thing that was different was that one of her dresses, a yellow cotton one, had fallen to the floor.

'What are we looking for?' she asked, picking up the dress.

'I don't know,' Gully said, 'but I don't like the sound of this visitor.'

Clemency felt another shiver coming on, and not just because of the cold bedroom air.

'Why not?' she asked, in voice that came out rather small.

'Because I don't think she was theatre folk after lodgings. I don't think she was after lodgings at all. I think she was after *you*.'

'If they're after me, what are they after me *for*?' asked Clemency.

She sat with Gully over the kitchen fire, gazing into the red coals, listening to them click and fall to ash. Whitby was still at the theatre, Leicester was under the stairs, fixing his cart, and Aunt Hett had dozed off in her chair, apron askew and mouth half-open.

'After? I wish I knew,' Gully sighed. 'And I wish Ma were here; she'd have some good ideas. She'd get us thinking like detectives.'

'Do you believe that man—those men—were really watching us?'

Gully shook his head slowly. 'I dunno. There's been no sign of 'em today.'

'And this mysterious lady. What was she looking for in my room?'

Again he shook his head. 'Could they be from your family?'

'Then why didn't those men come right to the house? And why didn't this lady ask for me?'

'Perhaps they were sent to spy on you, find out if you were genuine. I mean, you might be an impostor trying to worm your way in.'

'Why would I do that?'

'For the money, of course!' said Gully, and grinned. 'The family riches.'

Clemency looked baffled. 'I'm only here because I've nowhere else to go. And we don't even know if there *are* any family riches.'

'Worse luck.' Gully knuckled his forehead, as if he might push the right answers into his brain. 'Just think, though—your parents are dead in India. No one here in England could say if you're the real Clemency Wrigglesworth—or even if Clemency Wrigglesworth exists.'

Clemency's jaw dropped open. 'But I'm not capable of tricking anyone. I'm just . . . well, just an eleven-year-old orphan. What harm could I do?'

'What harm indeed?' Gully chuckled. 'But you've set the cat amongst the pigeons somehow, somewhere. I can feel it, up here.'

And with one finger he tapped the space between his eyes.

Chapter 6
Money Troubles

—╫O╫—

Next morning Clemency found the parlour fire unlit, the table covered with no more than its brown plush cloth. She didn't mind. It would be warmer down in the kitchen; less lonely, too. As she came hesitantly down the basement stairs, Hetty, who was stirring the porridge, called out, 'Morning, Miss! You can come and help Leicester. He's making jam tarts.'

'Like this,' Leicester showed her, pushing the jam off the spoon with a grubby finger, then popping the jammy finger into his mouth.

'Don't use the same finger you licked!' cried Whitby, who was sitting at the cluttered table, leafing through a fashion paper.

Leicester went on to use his middle finger for the next jam tart, his third for the next, and his little finger for the next. After each manoeuvre he sucked the jam off. When he had used up all his fingers he started with his index finger again. Clemency watched him, then picked up two teaspoons and used one to scrape the jam off the other. She hoped she would be able to distinguish her jam tarts from Leicester's when they came out of the oven.

'That's a good girl, earning your keep at last,' Whitby said in an idle voice as if she was only thinking aloud. 'Ma can't keep you in parlour fires for nothin'. Can't have the best bedroom and feather counterpanes piled sky-high like the Princess and the bloomin' Pea, all for sweet tiddly-pom.'

Clemency concentrated on placing the jam exactly in the middle of each pastry circle, but she felt her cheeks burning and she bent lower over the table to hide them. Even the glass eye in its jar, still there from the night before, seemed to be watching her.

Whitby put down her paper and glared straight at Clemency. 'Got no money, yet she thinks she's the cat's whiskers.'

At that moment Gully came bounding down the stairs. 'Who's the cat's whiskers? Talking about yourself again, Whitby?'

'No, Miss Indian Memsahib here.'

Gully looked at Clemency's bent head and glowing face.

'She's not an Indian memsahib, she's just a kid,' he said, his voice breaking on a squeak of indignation at the word *kid*. 'And I'll thank you to remember she's my mother's guest here.' He had put on his grandest tone.

Clemency felt her cheeks begin to cool.

'Ma's subbed Aunt Hett enough to cover her stay so far, so put that in your pipe and smoke it, Whitby Marvel!'

The last words didn't sound so grand, but Clemency could have hugged him.

'I just hope your little investment pays off in the end,' Whitby said, gathering up her paper, swishing her skirts, and waltzing off up the stairs.

Clemency bit at her thumbnail. So that's what Mrs Potchard meant when she said 'to defray expenses here'. How could she have been so dense, sitting there and listening and innocently asking Gully how he made his living? What must they have thought of her? But she had never had to worry about money before—money for jam, and leek pies, and coal, and who paid the cabman for the ride. And the newspaper for printing her advertisement! She was used to all these things being taken care of without question. So, Mrs Potchard had quietly used her fee for delivering the twins to pay for Clemency's food and lodging, in the rather distant hope of being rewarded by her family, when they were found. *If* they were found, as Whitby seemed to suggest.

'Oh dear,' said Clemency. It explained a lot. The Marvels and the Potchards had only themselves to do all the work in the pokey little house, and they had to earn money, by taking other people's children from place to place, or finding things that were lost. And Whitby wasn't dancing at the theatre just for fun.

But all these thoughts came into her head in a jumble, and she couldn't have expressed them out loud. She just stood there, blushing all over again, and repeating, 'Oh, dear.'

'Don't give it a thought, old girl,' said Gully, in a plummy voice just like Colonel Hibbert's. 'Cousin Whitby and I've had many a spat, and we're always friends again in a trice.'

But Clemency couldn't tell him that that was *not* what she was worrying about. To change the subject she leaned closer to Gully and whispered, 'Tell me something. Whatever is that glass eye doing on the table?'

Gully burst out laughing. He didn't bother to keep his voice down. 'It belongs to Mr Grigg. He's Aunt Hett's best lodger. He has a glass eye, and a couple of spares, and he must have left this one behind. She's keeping it until he comes back. He's a commercial traveller and he's often in town.'

'But why is it here in the kitchen?'

'I said he's Hetty's best lodger. Usually he stays in the best room—the first-floor front. But we didn't think you'd like an eye staring at you from the dressing table, so we brought it down here.'

Clemency eyed the eye, and felt an unstoppable giggle rising up inside her chest. And she felt light-hearted for the first time in days.

After breakfast Hetty helped Clemency to look through her mother's luggage.

'Hadn't your ma got any jewellery?' she wanted to know. 'That's always the best to sell.'

'She did have, but I don't know what happened to it.'

Hetty tutted softly. 'They say she died, in Bombay,' she murmured, as if she was talking to herself.

Clemency winced. Mrs Potchard must have filled Hetty in on the facts. Captain Christmas must have filled Mrs Potchard in. Clemency hated it when other people talked about her. She wished her mother had never given them the excuse.

'In the hotel?' Hetty went on, gently.

'No, not in the hotel. She ran into some old friends, and went to stay with them. That's when she became ill, at their house.'

'You were lucky not to catch it, too.'

'I couldn't have caught it there. She left me behind, at the hotel, so that I wouldn't spoil her fun.'

Hetty's mouth pursed into a thoughtful circle. But she didn't say anything else. Until a moment later, when she felt inside one of the silk pockets of the trunk and pulled out a small beaded case.

'Ah, what have we in here? A watch, I do believe! Your dear departed pa's watch and chain?'

'Yes,' said Clemency. 'It must be.'

Hetty glanced at her and then back at the watch. 'Is he long gone, then, your pa?'

'Last spring. That's why we were coming back to England. He fell from his horse.'

That's what she had learned to say, by copying Mama. She didn't say that he had been in a race with another officer, for a bet, and his horse had crashed over a fence and couldn't get up, and Colonel Hibbert had to shoot it to put it out of pain. Papa's horse had terrified Clemency. It was so big and black, always stamping and rolling its eyes and looking to see if it could bite someone. But she didn't wish it dead. *How typical of the man*, Mama had cried when she heard the news. *Broke both their necks—over a stupid bet!*

Hetty's voice brought her back to the present. 'Now there's a dreadful thing,' she was saying, apparently talking to the watch, 'to lose both Ma and Pa in the twinkling of an eye.'

Clemency didn't reply. She had felt more miserable about leaving her ayah, the Indian nursemaid who laid out her clothes, and brushed her hair, and put her to bed every night. '*Of course we cannot take her to England with us*,' her mother had said. '*Don't look at me like that, she's only a servant. You will barely notice she's gone.*' Oh, won't I? Clemency had thought.

Hetty tucked the watch into her apron pocket and shut the lid of the trunk. 'This will fetch a bit. Nothing else of use, though. Not a sausage.' And she shook her head sadly.

Hetty took Clemency's arm in a sharp grip as they set out from Wentworth Gardens.

'We'll pop the watch first.'

Clemency had no idea what she meant. They stopped at a cross between a jeweller's and a clockmaker's and a musical instrument shop, with a few old coats and shoes piled up at the back. Hetty muttered with the man behind the counter, then passed over Papa's watch in exchange for a handful of coins and a ticket.

'Keep a hold of that ticket,' she instructed. 'Then, if you come into money, you can redeem your pa's watch.' She gave Clemency a sharp look. 'Never pawned anything before, have you? Never had to. Ooh, the luxury of being rich!'

I never knew that I was, Clemency thought.

'You hand over your valuables and you get a loan. It's like a poor man's bank.'

'What about those coats and shoes?'

'They're the most valuable thing some folk have got.'

Before Clemency could think of a reply, Hetty pinched her arm again and propelled her out of the door. They scurried on, into a draper's shop. Hetty picked at rolls of fabric, scrabbled through drawers of gloves, and perched hat after hat on Clemency's head. She fixed her with a dissatisfied stare.

'Now, *that*, on my Whitby, would look ever so smart.'

She twitched the last hat off again and sighed. But it was wrapped, along with the other purchases, and they hurried back to Wentworth Gardens.

Gully was keen to see what they had got for their money, so Clemency unwrapped the dark-blue dress material, and the plain grey cape.

'You'll look a very meek and modest girl when you go calling on your relatives in that get-up,' he said.

'I think that's the plan,' Clemency murmured.

'Ooh, what a dreary colour.' Whitby picked up the dress material disdainfully, then remembered something. 'I say—you'll never guess what.'

She paused dramatically, so that they would have to ask, '*What?*'

'I enquired around about that ladies' orchestra, the one Leicester scared away. No one's heard of 'em, not a peep. Not booked to play anywhere in town. I think that boy made it all up.'

Gully looked dubious. 'Someone made it all up,' he said, 'but it certainly wasn't Leicester.'

A second advertisement appeared in *The Times,* but still nothing came of it.

'Time to send that letter,' Gully decided. 'Direct to the Great Hall, Caredew. That's what Ma told me to do. So let's not waste any more time.'

Clemency agreed. 'Good,' she said, in a determined voice.

Gully added, 'Whitby can take it. She goes right past the big post office on her way to the theatre. Then we can be certain the letter will get there safe and sound.'

The thought of the letter arriving made Clemency's heart beat faster, though whether with excitement or fear she couldn't be sure.

By now she was ready to meet her relations. Hetty had made up a very neat dress out of the blue material; there was the cape with matching gloves, and the hat that Hetty had chosen. Clemency was upstairs trying it all on when she heard someone rapping loudly on the front door. She peered out of the bedroom window, but couldn't see anything because the porch roof overhung the doorway below. A scuffling and a thumping in the hall announced Leicester's arrival to answer the door. Next she heard him call for Whitby, the only other person in the house. There followed a short conversation in low voices, and then Leicester ran up to her room. Clemency beat him to the door and opened it eagerly.

'You're wanted below.'

'Who is it?'

'A lady. She's askin' for you.'

At last, she thought, someone has come, someone has really come. 'What is she like?'

Leicester shrugged.

In an instant Clemency forgot any previous worries. Her head filled with visions of someone who looked like her mother, fair-haired and elegant, with a hat decorated with roses, and a delicate parasol, and wafts of scent. It could be an aunt or a cousin; there could be a whole gaggle of relations in Somerset, all kind and attentive, and dying to meet her. She pushed past Leicester, the thoughts crowding her imagination so brightly that she didn't see the dingy landing and the dark stairs at all. She flew down to the parlour. The door stood half-open. A flash of lavender satin was visible through the gap, but she realized that this was only Whitby's skirt. She paused, took a deep breath, and pushed open the door.

Whitby turned round to her and said, 'Oh, there you are. Clemency—this is Miss Clawe.'

Chapter 7

Miss Clawe

Miss Clawe was tall and thin and dressed in deepest black. Her hair was salt-and-pepper grey, scraped back from her face so fiercely that it pulled her eyebrows up into high arches. She wore an old-fashioned bonnet over it, festooned with black satin ribbons. And she carried—not a parasol—but a black umbrella, tightly furled.

'Miss Wrigglesworth?' Miss Clawe narrowed her eyes and inspected Clemency from head to foot.

'Yes,' said Clemency, with a sigh. This was what I was really expecting all along, she thought. Not ringlets and roses and parasols. The Potchards and the Marvels had turned out so unexpected that I forgot. But what I really thought would lie in wait for me was someone just like Miss Clawe.

'If you wouldn't mind, Miss Marvel,' Miss Clawe said to Whitby, giving her an eagle-like stare. Whitby, transfixed, backed out of the room without a word and carefully shut the door.

'Miss Wrigglesworth.' Miss Clawe's words drummed out like orders, instead of questions. 'Your parents are dead.'

'Yes.'

'Their names were.'

'Captain Wrigglesworth. And Mrs Wrigglesworth. Lucie.'

'Previously what.'

'I beg your pardon?'

'Her name was previously what. Before her marriage.' Miss Clawe sounded exasperated. Clemency felt stupid and slow-witted. It reminded her of her lessons back in India, of the way her governess would ask a question and wait, tapping her ruler impatiently, while Clemency struggled to come up with the right answer.

'I don't know.'

'You don't know!'

'Mama never mentioned it.'

'It was Lestrange.'

Was it? Clemency had never heard that name. Mama must have been Lucie Lestrange before she married Papa. She felt like saying, '*If you knew, why did you ask me?*' But she knew that you didn't do that sort of thing with creatures like Miss Clawe.

'I am housekeeper to your aunt. You are to come with me to the Great Hall.'

At least *she's* not my aunt, Clemency thought.

Miss Clawe held up her hand, as if to call for silence. Did she just read my mind? Clemency wondered, horrified. But Miss Clawe simply walked to the parlour door and wrenched it open. Whitby stood right outside, her nose almost touching the door panel.

'Oh—er—,' she stammered. 'I was just comin' to ask if you would care for a cup of tea.'

Miss Clawe nodded curtly, and waited, watching, as Whitby hurried down the kitchen stairs. Leicester, who was halfway up them, got spun around like a top and thrust back down again.

Miss Clawe glanced at Clemency. 'You are ready.'

Unfortunately, Clemency was. She had on her new dress, her gloves and hat; even the cape, which she had forgotten was flung around her shoulders.

'Come, then.'

'But what about the tea you just—?'

'We must make haste,' Miss Clawe said coldly.

Clemency realized that she was about to leave Wentworth Gardens and that neither Gully nor Mrs Potchard were there to say goodbye. But it was too late. Miss Clawe grasped her furled umbrella in one hand and Clemency's elbow in the other, and marched her out into the gathering gloom of the November afternoon.

'Where've they gone!?' Whitby almost dropped the tea tray. She gawped at the empty room. 'Less-STAH!'

When Leicester appeared, she demanded, 'Did you see 'em go?'

'No, Sis.'

'Did you hear 'em?'

'Not a squeak.'

'Quick, see if you can spot 'em down the street.'

Leicester rushed to the front door and, finding nothing, scrambled up to the first floor. Whitby heard his boots above her, then clumping down the stairs again.

'Nuffing, Sis. No one. Not a soul.'

Whitby stood on the threshold of the parlour, frozen to the spot with astonishment. 'Vanished—just clean vanished! And me with their tea set out so dainty.'

'What about them boxes of Miss Clem's?' Leicester asked. The effort he'd made getting them into the house had clearly left its mark on him.

'They're still upstairs?'

'Course they are.' He pulled back his shoulders and threw out his chest. 'It'd take a *perfessional* to get 'em down. And that Miss Clawe never asked me.'

Whitby slammed the tea tray down on the table, caring nothing now for daintiness, and put her hands on her hips.

'And what about our money? The spiky old bat just grabbed young Clem and done a flit. However am I going to explain *that* to Ma?'

Gully frowned. 'Gone without so much as a goodbye? That doesn't sound like her.'

'No, it don't,' Hetty agreed. 'Young Miss Clem had manners, I'll give you that.'

'Well, she's gone, and that's all I know,' Leicester told them firmly, folding his stubby arms across his chest.

He was in no mood for further interrogations. 'You'll have to wait for Sis to come home from the theatre if you want to know more.'

Feeling troubled, Gully kept to his attic all evening, reading a dull book, and getting very cold, which somehow suited his bad mood. Hetty busied herself in the kitchen. She was burning with curiosity to hear what Whitby had to say.

They both heard Whitby come down the street late that night. Gully, high up in the house, heard two pairs of footsteps, two low voices, and Whitby's hoarse laugh. Hetty heard her run down the area steps in her high-heeled shoes, bang on the window as she went by, and fling open the door, letting in a swirl of foggy air. By then both Gully and Aunt Hett were there on the spot to greet her.

'Tell us all about it!' they cried.

'Oh, Ma, you'll never guess!'

'Yes, we will,' said Gully, and Hetty said, 'Go on, then!'

'Oh, Ma, you've got to say yes. You've got to let me go.'

'Go where? What's this?'

'They're touring all round the West Country, and then on up North. Oh, please, please, *please*!'

Hetty's mind turned over several ideas, none of which made sense.

'I know you'll understand. I might be a Marvel, but underneath I'm a Potchard.'

'*What!?*' said Gully.

'The Red Indians,' Whitby said, as if that explained things.

'What have they got to do with Clemency?'

'*Clemency?*'

'The Red Indians?' Hetty prompted.

'Oh, Ma! I've just told you!' Whitby sat down in a huff, her crimson skirt and many petticoats floating out over the chair and settling slowly.

'Whitby, who are the Red Indians?' Gully gently tried asking. 'And what have they got to do with—?'

'They asked me yesterday, and they asked me again tonight, and you've got to let me,' she whined, sounding just like Leicester. Her stage make-up had streaked over one eye, giving her an angry, lopsided frown.

'Who?' Hetty sat down too, brushing wisps of hair out of her tired eyes.

'The Red Indians, the Genuine Red Indians, asked me to go on tour with them. One of them's off,' here she dropped her voice, 'with a *confinement*, and they need another girl to fill in. And they asked *me*. Oh, do let me go, Ma! You know how it feels to want to be off on the road. And he says I look just like a *real* Red Indian, with my black hair and all.'

'Ah, now we have it, my girl!' Hetty said. 'Who's the *he* you seem so keen on listening to?'

'One of the Red Indians . . . his name's Little Hawk.'

Hetty looked sceptical. 'I don't know what your father would've said.'

'I do! He'd have said, *Off you go, girl, and good luck to you. It's in your blood, travelling round and doing shows.*'

'Well, being a Red Indian's not in your blood, however much you think you look like one,' Hetty told her. 'And we didn't stay up so late just to hear all this nonsense. What about young Clem, and this Miss Clawe? And did you get our money?'

'Oh, Ma!' Whitby slumped sulkily in her chair.

'You know Leicester couldn't tell you the facts if he was reading them off the railway timetable,' said her mother. 'I want to hear it properly.'

'From beginning to end,' added Gully.

So Whitby recounted Miss Clawe's visit, with a full description, and everything she had gleaned from pressing her ear to the parlour door.

Gully said, 'So Clemency has an aunt at Caredew.'

Hetty murmured, 'I hope they *do* settle up. Those that can afford it ten times over, they're always the worst payers.'

'She must have come because of the letter,' Gully said.

Whitby went red in the face and shot up out of her chair, hand to her mouth. She grabbed her coat and began fumbling in the pockets.

'What is it?' asked Gully.

She pulled out a crumpled envelope and handed it to him without a word.

He smoothed it out. 'The letter Ma left.'

'I forgot to post it,' Whitby confessed. 'I've been carrying it about, but with all this excitement over the Red Indians I clean forgot. I walked there and back with Jerry—you know, Little Hawk. We was talking all the way and I just forgot.'

Gully handed the envelope to his aunt. 'So they must have seen the advertisement, instead. Did she say so, this Miss Clawe?'

Hetty stared at the envelope and turned it over. 'You shouldn't've opened it, Whitby. Even if you did know what's inside, it's still none of your business.'

'I didn't open it, Ma. I just forgot to post it.'

'The seal's broken.'

Gully leaned over Hetty's shoulder. He lifted the flap and looked inside. 'No letter.' He glanced up at his cousin, who was no longer red in the face and guilty-looking, but pale and obstinate.

'*I* didn't open the letter and *I* didn't take it out! If I'm honest enough to own up about not posting it, why would I lie about that? It don't make sense.'

Gully frowned. 'No, it doesn't. Who could've taken it? We've got no lodgers other than Clemency.'

'And we haven't had any visitors,' said Hetty.

'Yes, we have. That woman Leicester showed around. Miss Lysander, was that her name?'

'The one with a whole orchestra . . .' Hetty said faintly.

'We ought to ask Leicester.'

'Oh, the poor boy,' Hetty protested, but Leicester was summoned, sleepy and tousled, from his bed in the attic.

'I don't know nuffing,' he said in a grumpy voice, his eyes still closed. He put his head down on the kitchen table and prepared to go back to sleep. 'I 'aven't seen no letter.'

'So, Ma wrote the letter,' Gully spoke his thoughts aloud, 'and left it on the parlour mantelpiece, and sometime after that Miss Lysander called, and then Whitby took the envelope and put it in her pocket.'

'And forgot to post it, I know. And now here it is, seal broken and no letter inside,' Whitby concluded for him.

'Was Miss Lysander ever alone in the parlour?'

'No,' Leicester muttered, peevishly, from the table-top. His mother reached out and stroked his tangled hair. 'No, I stuck to her like glue, even when she was tryin' to get up the stairs without me. I never left her anywhere alone.'

'Can you recall what she looked like?' Gully asked.

Leicester recited, without lifting his head, 'Short. Stocky. Mole on her nose. I *tole* you before. Very particular sort. Kept fussin' in the mirror.'

'The mirror in the parlour? The mirror over the mantelpiece? So she *could* have snitched the letter. I wonder why? And who is she, really?' Gully asked, gazing at Whitby.

She gazed back with gleaming eyes. 'And Miss Clawe,' she added. 'She could be anybody, too. She didn't show me nothin' to prove who she was, or where she come from. She just whisked Clemency out from under our noses, didn't she, Less?'

Denied the drama of her Red Indians, she was beginning to enjoy the drama of Miss Clawe.

'Ooh, dear,' said Hetty slowly. 'What's your Ma going to make of this when she gets back from France?'

Gully shook his head. 'And what's more, she left *me* in charge.'

Chapter 8
A Little Experiment

---⊩○⊩---

Gully Potchard had hardly slept at all when the late November dawn poked its way in through his attic window. He'd spent the long dark hours worrying about Miss Lysander and Miss Clawe, and just what had happened to Clemency. Sometimes he was able to tell himself that there was nothing sinister in it all, and his mother would say the same when she came home. But when he rolled over and tried to sleep, his worst fears came vividly into mind, making sleep impossible. There is never such a bad time to think about worrying things as in the middle of the night, for there is no one to talk to and no bright daylight to make things seem less fearful. What made it worse was that Leicester slept soundly, and snored loudly, in the next bed.

By breakfast time, Gully had made up his mind to escape his problems by running away to sea. Perhaps Captain Christmas would give him a job as a cabin boy. But then Ma would as likely as not turn up on board, and that would be no escape. Next he thought he would try to get to Somerset to find out if Miss Clawe was genuine and whether Clemency was safe with her loving family. But he hadn't a penny to his name to get him there, and nor had anyone else in the household, except perhaps Whitby.

Whitby was never a good person to approach in the mornings. She was by temperament a night-time person. Working late into the evening exhausted her, and larky as she might be at midnight, at eight the next day she was murder.

'I've just *got* to have a loan,' Gully began. 'You must see how I'm placed. When Ma finds out I've messed everything up, she'll never forgive me. I've got to put it right before she gets back.'

'No,' said Whitby, turning over in bed and showing him her back.

'You're the only one with a sou to lend. Please, Whitby.'

'No!'

'It's partly your fault, anyway. You let that witchy Miss Clawe take Clem—'

'No, no, NO!' screamed Whitby, sitting up. 'And what do you think you're doing in my room? Get out!'

'Oh, go on, Whitby, you know you feel bad about it too . . .'

'GET OUT!' Whitby yelled, picking up a shoe and making ready to throw it. Gully decided it was time leave. Before he could shut the door, the shoe hit him squarely between the shoulder blades.

'What were you going to do with the Red Indians—knife throwing?' he called back at her. 'They've missed a good 'un there.'

'It's still not too late,' she shouted in reply. 'And why don't you use your bloomin' psychic powers to call up Miss Fancy-pants Wrigglesworth, if you're such a know-all? Because any money I've got is going to poor Ma, after all her trouble, not to you, you . . .'

But Gully didn't stay to hear what she called him. He slammed the door and ran downstairs.

In Clemency's room her trunks stood around, half-unpacked where Aunt Hett had rummaged through them. There were her airy summer dresses, her white shoes, her straw hats. There was a doll with brown curls and staring eyes, but he'd never seen Clemency touch it, so it couldn't be very important to her. He was looking for something that summed her up, something that was dear to her. The equivalent of a dog's lead or a cat's bell, something she used or wore every day. Finding nothing in her room, he went to look for Aunt Hett. He had an idea. He needed some of the blue material she had made up into the dress for Clemency. She was wearing that dress when she left, and she would still be wearing it now. It might do very well.

He found Hetty in the parlour sweeping out the grate.

'Should've done this yesterday,' she was muttering. She always buried herself in hard work when times were difficult.

'Where's the remains of that stuff you made into Clemency's dress?'

'Why, what d'you want it for?' Hetty sounded suspicious.

'A little experiment. I want to see if I can *see* where she is and if she's all right, and I need a bit of her dress material to do it.'

Hetty got up stiffly. She flicked at the ashes on her apron with a hand so dirty it just left further marks.

'Do you really need that stuff? Only I got a use for it myself. If you want something of hers, why don't you take this? Just found it on the floor.' And she handed him a crumpled handkerchief. 'See, it's got her initial embroidered on it. Surely that'd do?'

Gully smoothed out the square of white cotton. In one corner was a fancy W worked in satin stitch. 'I can try. Thanks, Auntie.'

He went back up to the attic where he could be alone and concentrate. He cupped the scrap of cotton in his hands, closed his eyes, and thought hard. He had a routine for this sort of thinking. First he tried to clear his mind of everyday thoughts, such as the cold draught from the attic window and how icy his feet felt. Then he tried to shut out the surroundings he had just closed his eyes on, and to see only a dull dark nothingness instead. The colour he favoured for his dull darkness was a rich chocolate-brown. When he had achieved that, he began to concentrate on the thing, or in this case the person, he wanted to *see*. He clutched the handkerchief and made himself picture Clemency in her new dress and cape and hat. He let her image sink into the chocolate darkness in his mind. It was very difficult. She kept disappearing. He tried to bring the darkness back, but nonsense thoughts intervened. In the end he snapped open his eyes, and gave up.

He went down to the front door to survey the grey and wintry morning.

'Any luck?' asked Hetty, who was on her knees cleaning the front steps.

'No, nothing.'

'Maybe it's not a very *psychical* time of the day?'

'Mmm,' said Gully, doubtfully.

Hetty stood up, her knee joints cracking. 'This cold gets into my bones.'

'Poor Aunt Hett. But I'm sure things'll look up soon.'

'Yes—they'll look up the chimney and find it's black, that's all.'

Behind her, someone was putting his big muddy boot on the bottom step. She grabbed her box of cleaning rags angrily, sweeping it out of the way. Then she glanced back, to see a drab-looking gentleman very much like a walrus. Her anxious face broke into a wide, welcoming beam.

'Oh, Mr Grigg! 'Ow delightful to see you again!'

Hetty's best lodger had returned. Mr Grigg nodded

good morning to her, twinkling at her with his good eye whilst fixing Gully sternly with his glass one.

By midday Whitby was quite human again. Her insults had inspired Gully, and now she was as keen as he was to find out more.

'Try again,' she urged him. 'Try it in her room. That might help.'

Gully said, 'Leicester's in there, clearing her trunks out of Mr Grigg's way. Can't you hear him?'

'I thought it was elephants rehearsin' a circus act. Well, try the parlour. She spent a deal of time in there, gazin' into the coals.'

'Right-oh,' said Gully, and they both hurried up the kitchen stairs.

There was no fire in the grate, and the furniture had been pushed back so that Hetty could sweep. Whitby drew the curtains so that the room was even gloomier, and Gully settled in the armchair, clutching the handkerchief and trying to think. Whitby knelt on the hearthrug and watched him intently.

'Don't breathe so loud,' he told her, after a minute, then, crossly, 'It's all nonsense. It's not working.'

'No, don't open your eyes,' Whitby said. 'It may not be nonsense. Keep thinking. What do you see?'

'Well—I try to picture Clemency but she keeps slipping away. I see a kind of cloud, and a view.'

'But that's something, Gully. Keep trying. What kind of view?'

'It's like looking down a street . . . nearest is a bit of garden with railings round it . . . then the street going farther away. Tall houses, a sign sticking out. It's all a bit dim and grey.'

'Tell me about the sign.'

'Blue, square . . . an inn sign. White moon, sickle-shaped. Gold writing.'

'It sounds like the Sickle Moon in Aunt Troy's street!' Whitby squeaked in disbelief, clutching Gully's knees with her sharp fingers.

Gully opened his eyes wide, dropped the hankie, and lost the picture at once.

'Ow, you're hurting! Let go.'

'It sounded just like the Sickle Moon,' Whitby repeated.

'It was much clearer with you asking me questions. It was like you were leading me down into the picture, and I could see more and more.'

'So where was it? Are you any nearer knowing?'

'No. But once you said Sickle Moon, the picture on the signboard made sense. It was blurry, sort of foggy before. Only then you pinched my knees and I lost it all.'

'How many places are there in England with inn signs like the Sickle Moon?'

'Goodness knows. But you're right, it was just like Aunt Troy's street, if you looked at it from the other end, from across the square at the top.'

'Maybe it was,' said Whitby. 'Maybe that's where she is right now.'

Gully looked down at the screwed-up handkerchief, and breathed hard. He found *seeing* a bit frightening sometimes. 'What's she doing in London? I thought they'd taken her to Somerset.'

'Maybe they've packed her straight off to school. Sent her to Aunt Troy's revered establishment!' Whitby, overcome by the experiment's success, began to laugh.

'But it wasn't like looking from Aunt Troy's house. I told you, it was from the other direction.' Gully didn't feel like laughing. His mind was turning over possibilities, but none of them made him at all happy.

Chapter 9

At the Sign of the Sickle Moon

—⊢○⊣—

Leicester had something to celebrate. He spent much of his day wandering around the streets with his homemade cart. Sometimes he was able to help people shift things, as he had with Clemency's trunks, and get a penny or two in exchange. Sometimes he was able to find wood or scrap metal, which he could sell. If he felt daring he could wander around the docks or the markets where there were rich pickings to be had, but these pitches tended to be run by boys far tougher than him, and although he was well-built and strong he was too disorganized to be any good in a fight. Generally he stayed away from places like that.

But this afternoon, roaming through a particularly muddy part of town, his eye had fallen on something gleaming in the gutter, just before a set of wheels ran

over it. When the wheels had gone, Leicester, quite accustomed to mud, felt around with his bare hands and
soon found a hard, round shape. He picked it out and
shone it on his sleeve. And held up a glistening half-
sovereign.

Now he came whistling down Wentworth Gardens,
trundling his cart behind him and tossing the coin up
before his eyes with one hand, enjoying the sight of it
shining and spinning through the air.

Gully, sitting on Aunt Hett's newly whitened step,
saw him from far off. 'Leicester, my good man!' he
called out. 'When's a rich cove like you going to treat a
poor boy like me? Lend us a bob, Leicester.'

'I found it,' Leicester said proudly. 'I didn't even have
to earn it.'

'Remember how you helped us with that mystery
last night, Leicester?' Gully went on. 'I need some money
urgently, for matters pertaining to that. Matters of
national importance.'

'I can't split it,' Leicester said, looking pained. 'It's
all I got.'

'But it's a matter o' life and death.'

Leicester looked fondly at his coin. He had already
spent it many times over in his imagination. Sometimes

he had given it to his mother and gladdened her heart, and sometimes he had kept it himself and gladdened his own. But it was the work of a moment to decide, and he sent it spinning up in the air again for Gully to reach out and catch. 'What's it for?' he asked.

'You're a scholar and a gentleman, Leicester Marvel! I'll remember you in me will,' Gully said, already beginning to hurry away.

'But where're you off to?'

'Ask Whitby. She knows. She'll explain.'

Leicester stood on the doorstep, watching the dwindling figure run down the darkening street. His emotions were divided between glowing generosity and terrible regret. But Gully's repeated cry of 'A scholar and a gentleman!', echoing down Wentworth Gardens, gave him great comfort.

Aunt Troy was Dorothea Potchard's elder sister. She had been named Helen, after Helen of Troy, by a sentimental father gazing down at his firstborn. But it soon became apparent to everyone, even her mother and father, that wars would not be fought over this girl's beauty. She had a large hooked nose, tremendous eyebrows, and a well-developed jaw. They took to calling her Troy, instead of Helen, and the name stuck. Troy Porter, when full grown, was a formidable creature. She became a teacher and eventually opened her own school.

Miss Porter's Academy for Young Ladies occupied a rambling, shambling house in Squat's Lane, in an old-fashioned and unimproved part of London. Gully had often stayed there when his mother was away on one of her long journeys. Aunt Troy was the only member of the Porter–Potchard clan not to suffer from the travelling itch, and she was glad to have Gully for his longer stays. It gave her the opportunity to instil a little proper learning into his head, rather than magic tricks and travellers' lore.

To say that Miss Porter's Academy was for Young Ladies was something of an exaggeration, for they were not young *ladies* when they arrived, and not all of them had been turned into young *ladies* by the time they left. Miss Porter had a reputation for educating female children of the more disastrous sort—which to their families seemed very disastrous indeed. Girls were supposed to be like Clemency, timid and polite, neat and tidy, industrious and well-behaved; and when they weren't like this by nature, some of them were sent by their disappointed parents into Miss Porter's capable hands.

Miss Porter's method was to teach them to be neat and tidy and polite and industrious and well-behaved—but she refused to make them timid, as this wouldn't be of any use to them. With the more difficult girls, she taught them to *appear* to be well-behaved when it was necessary, so that they could impress their parents and other important people. At other times, she said, they could be just as horrid as they pleased, as long as it wasn't in her school. It was a very successful method, for most girls grew out of their horrible stage quite naturally, just as caterpillars become butterflies in time. And those that didn't, learnt to *act the part* of young ladies, and enjoyed themselves immensely. They even came back to the school as grown women, to thank Miss Porter for her efforts, and some of them winked at her as they did so.

It was late that night when Gully arrived at his aunt's house, and Miss Porter herself let him in.

'Gulliver! This is a surprise!'

'Hello, Aunt Troy. I hope I'm not disturbing you,' Gully said, in a rush. 'I've come all the way from Southampton on a most important matter.'

'Haven't stopped growing yet, I see.'

Gully blushed. Aunt Troy never hesitated to comment on matters he wished nobody had noticed.

Aunt Troy showed him into her small sitting room. Two King Charles spaniels raised their heads to give Gully the once-over, saw who it was, and went back to sleep. Gully clutched his cap in his hands, and stood before the fire, warming his frozen legs. 'I've come on business, so to speak,' he said.

'I don't know what *business* there can be between you and me, Gulliver,' replied Aunt Troy, settling back in her armchair and peering at him quizzically over the top of her spectacles. 'Except that you have a wayward daughter you wish me to educate. And I trust that will not be the case for some years to come, if ever.'

Gully ignored her teasing, took a deep breath and asked, 'Do you have a new pupil at your school called Clemency Wrigglesworth?'

'No.'

'Are you about to have a new pupil called Clemency Wrigglesworth?'

'No.'

'Have you been approached by anyone about taking a Miss Wrigglesworth?'

'No.'

'Or Lestrange?'

'No.'

'Or been approached by anyone called Lestrange?'

'No.'

'Or Clawe? A tall thin lady called Miss Clawe?'

'No.'

'Any tall thin ladies at all?'

'No.'

'Oh.'

There was a pause, during which Gully felt bitter disappointment, and also that the backs of his trousers were almost on fire. He moved away.

'My latest pupil came at the beginning of October and her name is Smith,' said his aunt. 'What is all this about?'

So Gully sat down and explained about Clemency and Miss Clawe, while Aunt Troy listened politely and yawned behind her hand. She had never believed in Gully's powers of seeing or finding things, largely because he had not found anything that she had lost. When his story was finished, she said, 'Well, there's nothing more to be done tonight, and I don't suppose you've had any supper. Go down to the kitchen and see what you can find, only let Ellen know it's you or she'll think you are burglar and knock you over the head with the frying pan.'

Gully woke up in an attic and at first couldn't think where he was. He knew it wasn't Wentworth Gardens because above him was a sparkling windowpane filled with bright blue sky. He climbed on the bed and looked out, to see acres of roofs white with frost, and thin plumes of smoke rising straight up in the air. And the tops of the bare trees in the square at the end of Squat's Lane. Which made him remember everything.

He dressed quickly and ran down the back stairs. Ellen and a kitchen maid were clearing away breakfast.

'You slept late,' Ellen said. 'But we kept some bacon warm for you.'

'I'll have it when I come back,' Gully cried, rushing past her. He grabbed a piece of fried bread as he went, stuffing it in his mouth and cramming his cap on at the same time. Outside he buttoned his jacket and pulled his cap down over his ears to keep out the freezing air.

Squat's Lane was a long street, curving uphill to the square at the end. He walked until he came to the public house on the corner, jutting out just where the square began. He stopped beneath the inn sign, then stepped back to get a better look at it. A blue-painted sign—white moon—gold writing. But this wasn't how it had been in his vision, as from here there was no view down Squat's Lane at all.

Gully crossed to the square gardens, a few scrappy bushes behind iron railings. Not right either. He crossed the road again to the far side of the square. He stationed himself outside the bookseller's on the corner, but from here he could see right down the lane, quite as far as his aunt's schoolhouse, and that was not what he remembered either.

He walked along a few paces to the sweetshop next door. Sugar mice and chocolate creams and cubes of coconut ice were arranged in tempting pyramids in the window. From here he could look right past the trees to Squat's Lane sloping away downhill, with the inn sign sticking out. The view was almost perfect. He pushed the door half-open, took a step inside, and peered out through its bay window. On either side were fine lace curtains tied back with pink ribbon. As he looked out, one of the curtains hung in a loop before his eyes. This was it! This was the strange cloud, the cloud through which he'd seen the street. Clemency must have stood here, and only yesterday!

A cough and a snuffle behind him made him freeze. In his eagerness he hadn't noticed whether there was anyone in the shop or not. Glancing back over his shoulder he made out a round head above the counter, a round red mouth with the end of a pencil stuck in it, and two round black currant eyes—staring straight at him.

The boy, for it clearly was a boy about Leicester's age, took the pencil out of his mouth. It made a popping sound.

'I can't serve you. I don't serve customers,' he said. His voice sounded bunged-up. He snuffled again. In front of him on the counter was an open ledger; Gully could see long neat lines of figures. The boy scratched his head with his pencil, wrote something down, then drew a line underneath it with an assured hand. 'I'm doing the accounts, if you want to know,' he said, carelessly. 'I've the best head for figures in the family. Father and Mother have handed this task entirely over to me. They say I have a Great Future.'

Gully could not imagine Leicester ever producing such a neat and painstaking page. Nor could he imagine Leicester sitting so calmly in a shop devoted to sweets. But then if the shop belonged to your mother and father you could probably help yourself to sweets any time you wanted—and the boy's round face and double chin showed that he had.

'I shouldn't really be interrupted in this work,' the boy went on. 'I'll call Mother.'

Gully, who hadn't interrupted in the first place, opened his mouth, trying to work out what he wanted to say.

'Can I help you, young man?' A woman stepped out through a curtain at the back of the shop. Her glance sized him up from top to toe.

Gully hadn't so much as a farthing in his pocket for sweets, no excuse to be in the shop at all, but he had a burning question. He became aware of his mouth flapping open and shut and no sound coming out.

'Do you want to make a purchase?' she continued, in a less obliging tone. 'Or are you just going to stand there *breathing* all over the confectionery?'

Gully blinked. The woman was short and stocky, with a square sort of face. There was a definite mole on her nose. She wore a plain dress, but she looked *very* particular.

He snapped shut his gaping mouth, shook his head, and backed out of the half-open door without uttering a single word.

Cold and hungry, Gully lurked in an archway beside the Sickle Moon. It gave him a good view of the sweetshop door. He had to find out more, and this was all he could think of: to do a little spying in return. After a very long wait, the sign inside swung round to 'CLOSED', and two figures stepped out, the boy and his mother. The boy, now that Gully could see the whole of him, was podgy in shape, buttoned into a tight overcoat and with a tasselled cap perched above his plump face. Gully watched the woman lock the shop door, then take the boy's hand and walk him briskly across the square.

He was about to follow them, when he noticed the signboard above the sweetshop for the first time. It said, in curly script:

Watkyn's High Class Confectionery

With a sinking heart, Gully reached into his pocket and pulled out a scrap of crumpled cotton. There was the same elaborate letter *W* embroidered in the corner. Not W for Wrigglesworth, but W for Watkyn! Leicester said their visitor had kept fussing in front of the mirror. She must have dropped the handkerchief when she was stuffing Ma's letter into her handbag. No wonder the image of Clemency kept slipping away when he tried to *see* her with it—the handkerchief was nothing to do with her. Which meant that she had never been here at all.

Gully didn't know whether to be cast down or elated. His mind raced, trying to make sense of it all. What was Mrs Watkyn from the sweetshop doing in Southampton, and calling herself Lysander? And why would she take such trouble to steal the letter and leave the envelope behind?

He stuffed the useless handkerchief back into his pocket and looked about him. There was no sign of Mrs Watkyn and her boy now, not in the square, nor down the little streets that ran off it. He slunk back to the Academy, where Ellen said, '*Breakfast?* You've got a hope, young man! We gave that bacon to the dogs.'

Aunt Troy was sitting at her high desk at the far end of the schoolroom. Gully looked at the bent heads of her pupils intent on their work, and crept down the side of the room. His stomach rumbled loudly. Several of the young ladies giggled. Just as he reached his aunt's desk, she uttered a single word. 'Out!'

He was forced to tiptoe back down the long room, holding his middle to keep it quiet and blushing a very deep red.

She found him in the hallway a few minutes later.

'What was the meaning of that display, Gulliver? Be quick, I have a lesson to teach.'

'I only wanted to let you know, as a matter of some urgency, that I found the place I saw in my mind, and a woman was there, the same woman who came to Aunt Hett's and lied to Cousin Leicester and stole a letter. I'm certain of it. It was *her* handkerchief Hett found, not Clemency's.'

'That *is* a coincidence,' Aunt Troy said, taking a sly glance at the fob-watch pinned to her jacket. 'Perhaps it requires some further investigation. In a purely scientific sense, of course. I can spare five minutes, no more.'

They went into her sitting room. Aunt Troy patted the spaniels while Gully described the events of the morning.

'Mr and Mrs Watkyn have run the shop there for several years,' Aunt Troy said. 'Their son is reputed to be a regular Boy Genius. Though I'm not sure I'd want to be responsible for his education. I hear he's rather spoilt.'

'I saw him. He was adding up the business accounts.' Gully expected his aunt to laugh, but instead she looked rather impressed. So he asked, 'Why would Mrs Watkyn pass herself off as someone called Lysander, who runs a ladies' orchestra?'

Aunt Troy came as near to shrugging her shoulders as such a dignified person ever could. 'That was simply a ruse to get into the house. As to the letter, you were all taken in. While the envelope sat there, you believed it was intact—there was no reason to suppose otherwise, in ordinary circumstances.'

'But these are turning out to be *extraordinary* circumstances, Aunt.'

'Your visitor did not know how soon the letter would be posted. By taking the contents of the envelope, Mrs Watkyn—if, indeed, it was she—could stop the news reaching its recipient at Caredew. Or, at the very least, delay it.'

'Stop someone from learning of Clemency's existence?'

Aunt Troy considered. 'That is mere speculation. We must stick to facts. But I will keep my eyes and ears open and see if I can come up with anything more. And now, I'm extremely busy, Gulliver. Is that all?'

Gully screwed up his face. 'Just one more thing, Aunt. Is there any possibility of lending me the fare back to Southampton?'

'Just this once, Gulliver, but please do not ask again. Not until you've paid me back. In full. And with one penny interest.'

Gully swallowed hard. Aunt Troy was the only person in the Potchard clan who had any money, and now he knew why.

Chapter 10
The Great Hall

━━◦━━

Clemency held her hat in her lap and gazed down at her gloves, which already looked grubby. Whoever was waiting for her at the Great Hall was so eager to meet her that they had sent a carriage for her. It couldn't get down Wentworth Gardens, but it had been waiting at the end of the street when Miss Clawe swept her out. They travelled long into the night, stopping before dawn for breakfast and to rest the horses. Miss Clawe didn't speak at all except to issue instructions.

Clemency was stiff with cold and sore from the endless jolting of the carriage. As the day lightened she stared out at her first view of the English countryside. The fields were muddy, the trees mostly leafless and black with rain. The sky was an unbroken blanket of grey. Rank smells wafted in through the draughty windows.

At long last the horses began to pick up speed, and Miss Clawe, who had been dozing, opened her eyes and glared about her. They swung through a great neglected gateway and down a long carriage road between huge trees. In the distance a steely lake reflected the sky. Beyond the trees a house came into view. A muddled-looking house—even Clemency, unused to English architecture, could see that—with towers and wings and chimneys and gables of every shape and colour. It was as if a child had tipped everything out of the brick-box at once, determined to use the lot to build a house, however strange the result.

'Is that the Great Hall, Caredew?' Clemency asked.

'It is,' replied Miss Clawe, tight-lipped. 'But that's no business of yours.'

Oh dear, thought Clemency. She tried again. 'Please, what is my aunt like?' Even if this person was her aunt's housekeeper, perhaps the aunt herself was nice and kind, and pretty and young.

Miss Clawe stared back at her. 'Your aunt. Why do you wish to know.'

'Because I—I—don't know anything about her, or my family in England. Mama never told me a thing.'

Mama never spoke to me much at all, she thought, except to criticize my hair, or my French accent, or the state of my handwriting.

'Your aunt is a very important person.'

'Oh.'

'Your aunt is not to be troubled.'

'No.'

'Your aunt is my business, not yours.'

Yes, thought Clemency, I'm beginning to understand that much.

They reached the house. Instead of following the broad drive round to the front, the carriage went under an archway at the side and into a yard. Clemency un-folded her stiff legs and climbed down. No one came rushing out to greet her.

'This way,' said Miss Clawe briskly, taking her through a plain door and down a stone-flagged passage.

A large woman in an apron stepped out of a door-way, and spotted them. A look of annoyance swept over her face.

'Your charge, Mrs Curd,' said Miss Clawe, pushing Clemency in the middle of her back so that she tripped forwards and almost fell against the large woman. 'My information is that she's a timid little thing.'

'Is this all, Miss Clawe? No luggage?' Mrs Curd asked, drying her hands on the skirt of her apron.

Miss Clawe made a face, as if she had tasted something nasty. 'Why would she need luggage,' she said, and hurried away up a twisting staircase.

'Welcome to Hilarity Hall,' the large woman said, with a flick of her eyebrow, when Miss Clawe was out of sight. 'Better follow me.'

The kitchen they entered was an enormous room, with a soaring ceiling and mountainous dressers and a scrubbed table as a big as the whole basement at Wentworth Gardens. A small girl in a white cap and apron was toiling away, carrying pots from one end of the room to the other, and, it seemed, carrying them back again.

'What work can you do?' Mrs Curd asked, surveying her kitchen rather than Clemency.

'Work?' said Clemency, in a small voice.

'If I'm to put you to work, I need to know what work you can do,' the woman explained, without much patience. Like Miss Clawe she sounded exasperated, but unlike Miss Clawe it seemed as if it was not people who exasperated her so much as circumstances. She didn't seem cross with Clemency, exactly, more the position she was placed in.

'I don't think I know any work,' Clemency tried. She hoped this didn't sound disobliging. It wasn't this woman's fault that Miss Clawe hadn't made things clear. 'I'm Clemency Wrigglesworth,' she explained.

Mrs Curd's expression didn't even flicker. 'You can be Clemency, Queen of the Fleas, for all I care. She's told me to put you to work, and I *will* find some work that you can do!'

At this outburst, the little scullery maid looked up and grinned. Clemency didn't think that it was a smile of fellow-feeling. It seemed more like sly enjoyment at her expense.

She turned her back on the girl and spoke in a low voice to Mrs Curd. 'I'm Clemency Wrigglesworth. My mother used to live here.'

'So did mine, and my pa too. Our family's been servants here as long as anyone can remember.'

'No,' said Clemency, whispering so fiercely she was almost hissing. 'You don't understand. My mother lived here as a girl. She was the daughter of the house. She was Lucie, who married Captain Wrigglesworth and went to India.'

Mrs Curd stepped back a pace, but instead of looking astonished or embarrassed, she put her fists on her broad hips and smiled an ugly smile.

'I said you might be Clemency, Queen of the Fleas for all I cared, and I meant it. Lucie Wrigglesworth don't exist here, nor no Clemency Wrigglesworth neither. So shut your trap, and keep it shut! You've got a lot to learn, little missy, and they won't be pleasant lessons. Now, if there isn't a single bit of work you can turn your hand to without teaching, you can get over there to Poll and beg her on your bended knees to learn you how!'

And with that she gave the astonished Clemency a flick around the head with her dishcloth that sent her spinning in the direction of the smirking little scullery maid.

Clemency peeled more vegetables than she had ever eaten, or seen, in her life. Vegetables whose names she didn't even know. Vegetables covered in mud, with thick knobbly skins that resisted the knife. Vegetables with *creatures* in them. Her hands turned red, and then blue, in the cold water. Well, now she knew how to peel vegetables.

At least the supper she had that evening was hot and substantial. It warmed her and made her feel more hopeful, if rather sleepy. Someone would send for her soon. Someone would realize the mistake. Perhaps the aunt—who must be somewhere in this huge house—would begin to think that Clemency should have arrived by now. She did worry that her new blue dress was ruined, and that when she met her aunt she would indeed look a fright. She had been given a long, coarse apron to put on, but try as she might, she could not stop the cold, muddy vegetable water drenching her sleeves and splashing all over her dress.

Once supper was cleared away and washed up, she was given her cape and hat back and told to follow Poll. The scullery maid took a stump of candle and hurried along innumerable dank passageways, trying—it seemed to Clemency—to lose her on the way. Finally they came to a small, cold room.

'Is this it?' Clemency asked, horrified. It made the best bedroom at Wentworth Gardens look like a queen's boudoir. The floor was bare. There was a straw mattress in one corner, covered by what looked like a heap of rags. In another corner stood a wooden chair with a broken cane seat, and a chipped china jug was balanced on the bit of the seat that wasn't fraying.

'You're lucky I'm willin' to share with you,' Poll said.

She took off her apron and dress, tossed them over the back of the chair, and—still wearing her grimy petticoat—climbed into the heap of rags.

'G'night,' she said, carelessly, and blew out the candle.

In the pitch-darkness that followed, Clemency ran her hand along the wall until she found a corner, then slid down on to the floor and sat there with her knees up, hugging them with her arms. She pulled her cape around her, shivering, and pressed her face down on to her knees. Who *are* these people? she thought. And what on earth do they want with me?

But she was too angry to cry. If all she felt was exhausted and miserable and scared, she might have started crying and never, ever stopped. But she felt a terrible anger as well, and slowly it crept along her bones like flames until it warmed her right through, and finally she was able to sleep.

Chapter 11
Bad Dreams

'This is a right kettle of fish!' Mrs Potchard said. 'What *has* been going on in my absence? I wish I could trust you, Gully, to be a less enterprising boy.'

They were all in the kitchen at Wentworth Gardens. Leicester was cleaning the knives, Gully was cleaning the boots. Aunt Hett cut up some fish for supper, and Whitby buffed her fingernails with a bit of cloth. Only Mrs Potchard seemed to be doing nothing, but she was thinking very hard.

'So we've got no child, no cash, and no real assurance of her safety?' she summed up. 'And an even deeper mystery than before.'

'You should've smelled a rat when you first agreed to take her on,' Hetty muttered. 'Sheer foolishness, Dolly. Payment in advance, or nothing doing.

A woman of your age and experience ought to know that. Too eager to do a favour for that ship's captain, that's your trouble.' And she narrowed her eyes at Mrs Potchard knowingly.

'It all seemed above-board when I took her on. The poor child was already there, waiting in the Captain's cabin, looking so sad and wan. How could I have said no?'

'Never trust a man with ginger side-whiskers,' was all that Hetty would say.

'So what do we do now?' asked Gully.

'Has anyone sent for her trunks?' his mother asked.

'They're in the back bedroom, first floor,' said Hetty. 'Leicester couldn't get 'em any further without doing hisself a serious injury.'

'Or the walls,' Whitby added.

'You know,' Mrs Potchard began, 'I had an inkling of trouble when I read her mother's letters on board ship. I was looking for an address, or a name. The letters unsettled me, but I thought it was just that her mother must have had an unhappy life here in England.'

They sat for a while in silence, apart from the squeaking of Leicester's knives.

'I think I'll go and find those letters,' Mrs Potchard said finally.

'Get outta my room,' Whitby said. Gully took no notice, since this was her usual greeting when either he or Leicester came into her attic, and he strolled on in. 'She's not best pleased with you, is she, your ma?' Whitby added.

'No,' Gully said gloomily. 'But I've got an idea.'

'Not another one.'

'Where's that blue stuff of Clemency's your mother had?'

'It's here.' Whitby picked up a garment that lay with a heap of others on the bed.

'Oh, Aunt Hetty made it into a little waistcoat for you!'

'Yes. 'Orrible colour, isn't it?' Whitby began, and then looked guilty. 'Still, I could give it back to Ma. She could do with it. I've got more clothes than her, anyway.'

'Can I borrow it for a bit first?'

'What for?'

'To try a bit more *seeing*. With something that was really hers. Will you help me, Whitby? It was so much clearer last time when you helped.'

Whitby brightened. She made room for Gully on the bed, tucked the patchwork quilt around both their shoulders, and left him in peace for a few minutes to concentrate. Then she said, 'Can you see anything? Is it working?'

'It's all dark. Not my usual darkness, though.'

'Concentrate.'

'It's dark, but it's a bit lighter at the top.'

'The top of what?'

'The top of the room, or the place, that I'm in. Not really a room. It's very small.'

'Can you see anything where it's lighter?'

'I can see round things, row upon row. Shelves with round things on. Jars, I think. Round jars, full of dark stuff.'

'Is it a cupboard?' suggested Whitby, in a soft voice, not wanting to shatter Gully's vision like last time.

'It's cold, and it smells odd. The floor is cold and hard. Oh!'

He sat up and threw back the quilt. Whitby stared at him with large frightened eyes.

'Whatever is it?' she asked.

Gully sat for a moment, pulling dreadful faces. Then he said, 'I felt horrible. I suddenly felt absolutely horrible, cold and sad and lonely and frightened, all mixed up and very strong, like when you're having a bad dream and you can't wake up.' He stared at Whitby, seeing his fear mirrored in her face.

'Do you think that's what Clemency is feeling?' he asked her. 'My last imagining was just what that Watkyn woman would see when she stood in her shop with no customers to attend to and stared idly out of the window. I didn't feel anything much then. But this time I saw *and* felt.'

Whitby, who was very impressed, had no idea what they should make of this.

But Gully, still shivering at the memory of the feelings, said, 'There's only one thing for it. We must join the Red Indians.'

Clemency was woken by Poll roughly shaking her shoulder. She stretched out her aching arms and legs, feeling as if a cavalry regiment had ridden right over her. One night in a rattling carriage and the next on the floor had done nothing for her looks or her temper.

'Better comb your hair,' Poll said, stooping over the water jug to wash her face. 'Mrs Curd likes us clean and tidy. Oh Lor', look at your dress. Looks as though you slep' in it!' And she laughed unpleasantly at Clemency.

'What with? I haven't a comb or a brush.'

'I'll give you the loan of mine, then,' Poll said, holding out a comb with half its teeth missing. 'For a *small fee*. What shall we ask?' she wondered, running her gaze up and down Clemency. 'I know—the ribbon off your hat.'

'Oh, go on, then!' Clemency said, tearing off the ribbon band and throwing it across the room at Poll. I shall have nothing left by tomorrow if we go on this way, she thought. Why did Miss Clawe say I had no luggage? Has she not sent for my trunks? Why didn't they just put them in the carriage? Even thin summer dresses would be better than no spare dresses at all. And when she *did* get to meet her aunt—whenever that might be—she would look even more of a scarecrow than she had at Wentworth Gardens.

Clemency followed Poll down to the kitchen where she was shown how to light the fires, boil the water, and pour it into brass cans. These were put in a chute which had a shelf that could be hauled up to the next floor: they disappeared into the hands of unseen upstairs servants. Only after carrying out numerous backbreaking chores did Clemency get any breakfast. She slumped into a chair. 'I feel as if I've done a whole day's work already,' she sighed.

'Think that's work?' Poll sneered. 'That's nothing. Gotta be strong to be a scullery maid.'

'I never claimed I was one.'

'No, and you won't last long as one, neither.'

'What will happen to me, then?'

Poll shrugged. 'Fall in the fire. Fall down the well. Fall down dead of sheer tiredness. Last thing my big sister said to me was, get outta the kitchen, Poll, quick as you can. Scullery maids never last long.' And she wiped her runny nose on the back of her wrist, and dug into her porridge as if she was starving.

It was after breakfast that the trouble began. Clemency was set to wash the pans which had been used to cook eggs and kidneys and kedgeree. The pans were made of copper and very heavy to lift. Everything that had been cooked in them that morning seemed to be the sort of food that *stuck*. She and Poll had only had porridge and bread and butter, and to scrape off all this stuff that she hadn't eaten and other people had was quite repulsive.

But she tried her best. She was determined not to be beaten. Her best was not very good.

Mrs Curd came up behind her to inspect her work. The first Clemency knew of it was when she roared, 'Useless, girl, useless! Do them all again.'

She did them all again, banging her knuckles and scraping her skin raw. Her arms ached too, from hauling the heavy pots in and out of the high sink. Mrs Curd came back again. She had to look more carefully this time, peering inside the shiny saucepans, for Clemency, fuming with annoyance, had put all her energy into the work.

Mrs Curd ran a finger round the inside of a milk-pan, and drew it out with a tiny smear of white on it.

'Still useless, girl! Do them all again.'

Something inside Clemency boiled up and boiled over, just as unstoppably as the milk had in the pan. She felt it go. 'Of course I'm useless!' she shouted back at Mrs Curd. 'I wasn't brought up to this. You'd be useless too, if you had to play the piano or ride a polo pony or write a poem in French! And then see how you'd feel when someone shouted at you for it!'

Not that *she* could ride a polo pony, never having been given the chance, and French was her worst subject. But Mrs Curd wasn't to know that. Out of the corner of her eye Clemency noticed Poll drop her pot-holder. Her mouth hung open wide in shock.

Then Mrs Curd's huge hand descended on the scruff of her neck and Clemency was propelled forwards, out of the kitchen, down the stone-flagged passage, and through a green door. She fell forward on to the cold hard floor, and heard the door slam behind her and a key turn in the lock. For a moment she was shaken, her knees and elbows ringing with the bang they'd had from the floor. But the fury still raged like a thunderstorm inside her. She was angry at all the injustices of the past two days. This gave her the energy to push herself up, dust down her skirt and hands, and look about her.

The room was dark, but light came in from some air vents just below the ceiling. She could see shelves ranged all around, far higher than she could reach, all filled with jars. Jar upon jar of pickled and preserved foods; things she recognized and things she couldn't begin to name. The air was full of the strange smell of their preserving liquids, oils and syrups and vinegars of all shades of red and gold and brown.

She banged on the door, but she knew that no one would come, even if they could hear her. There was no latch or handle on the inside, only the empty keyhole. Suddenly she recalled what Mrs Potchard had told her onboard ship: 'You have *inner resources*, my dear.'

'I'll show them,' Clemency said to herself. 'I'm going to make the most of being shut in a store cupboard!'

She chose a jar of cherries from the lowest shelf and tried to open it. The lid was too wide for her small hands to get a good grip. It would not move at all. She examined the other jars within reach. They were all as big, if not bigger, and all fastened just as tightly. She nearly dropped a jar of pickled cabbage putting it back on the shelf. She couldn't imagine what kind of punishment she would receive for breaking that, and she didn't even *like* pickled cabbage.

In the end she gave up, and sat down on the cold floor and sucked her sore knuckles. If only Gully and Whitby and Leicester were here, what a feast we would have, she thought. They would be sure to find a way to open all these jars.

Time ticked slowly by. What little light there was began to fade, and still nobody came to let her out. She grew cold and hungry. Her bruised knees ached. The consoling idea of *inner resources* faded away to nothing. Every so often she heard footsteps outside in the corridor, but they always went past without stopping or even pausing by the larder door to listen. Not a soul in this house was giving her a thought. To comfort herself she pictured the family at Wentworth Gardens, and wondered what they were doing right now. She saw them busy and jolly together in the warm, steamy kitchen, imagining her—if they thought about her at all—embarked on a new life of luxury with her rich relations. And here she was, shut up in a dark, chilly, vinegary-smelling cupboard, with nobody in the world to care about her, and no idea of what was going to happen next. But she wouldn't cry, she just wouldn't!

At last she heard light, skittering footsteps that stopped outside. A key clinked at the lock, the latch clicked, and Poll's white face stuck itself round the door.

'You can come out now. There's spuds to peel and trays to set,' she announced. 'Old Mother Curd's got 'er hair back on, but you'd better watch out. She's not used to anyone answering back.'

And Clemency had the feeling that there was an admiring glint in Poll's eye.

Chapter 12
Finding Out

—┼┼O┼┤—

At Wentworth Gardens Mrs Potchard and Hetty Marvel sat knee to knee by the kitchen range, feeling very glum. Mrs Potchard read through Lucie Wrigglesworth's old, faded letters for the umpteenth time, sighing.

'What do you think?' she said, passing them over. The first, in a firm hand and ink which had faded to brown, said:

My Dear Lucie,

You may find this hard to believe, but your stepbrother and I are, for once, in complete agreement. Each of us has told our father in most forcible words __not__ to give his permission for this foolish marriage. My advice to you is to inform Capt. Wrigglesworth that you cannot possibly accept his proposal. *If you come home at once from Mrs Kent's you will no longer be in the company of Capt. W. and the memory of him will soon fade. Be ruled by your head, not your heart. Papa has always given in to your every whim, but to this, I can assure you, he will never consent.*

H. T. L.

Hetty read the letter through twice and said, 'Well, she didn't take H.T.L.'s advice, did she? She became Mrs Wrigglesworth, and good luck to her.'

'With or without her father's permission,' Mrs Potchard added. 'I hope she was happy with him if she married him in the teeth of such opposition. Now, read the other one.'

This letter was full of blots and crossings-out. The writing doubled back on itself to cover the tiny sheet of paper.

Dear Miss Lucie,

I have sent on your things as instructed. I ~~cot~~ could not fit all the boots, etc. into the tin trunk, but the box-trunk holds more than expected. Your two hat-boxes included. Miss Honoria continues in a fit—you know what her temper is like—even more so when she heard from Mrs Kent of yr. ~~elop~~ elopement.

123

I have not seen Mr Theo. He keeps to his rooms as usual.
Miss H. did get him to agree with her and they ~~plaiget~~ plagued
yr. poor papa to such an extent that he threatened to Shut
Up the house and go to London or somewhere, tho we know he
would never do it. Now he says the Little Hall will do. We are
all in a sorry state Miss, things is as bad as they old. be but
I hope you will not dwell on it. Those that love you send their
Best Wishes on the ~~seais~~ occasion of yr. marriage to Cpt.
Wrigglesworth and I have shed many tears at your going,
happy and sad. I could not find yr. blue umbrella anywhere.
        Yours, Molly

'I can't make head nor tail of them,' complained
Hetty. 'They're too much concerned with things we
know nothing about.'

'It's bad news, that's what,' said Mrs Potchard, firmly.
'I should have realized that long ago. I should have taken
that little girl to the very door and seen her safely into the
hands of some responsible person. There's a stepbrother
mentioned in the first letter. Clemency's step-uncle, that
would be. And "your poor papa" would be her grandfather, if he's still alive, and this Molly was obviously
Lucie's maidservant. But who H.T.L. is, I'm not sure.'

'Look, it says "our father",' Hetty pointed out. 'This

H.T.L. must be another brother or a sister or stepsister, or they'd never call him *our* father.'

'Well done, Hett, you're quicker than me. And this Miss Honoria who is mentioned—well, Honoria begins with an H.'

The kitchen door flew open as she spoke and Leicester appeared, pink-faced and dishevelled, though that was nothing unusual.

'A message just come from the theatre,' he said, holding out a note to his mother. She jumped up and snatched it from him but passed it straight to Mrs Potchard, saying, 'You read it, Dolly. I can't look! It'll be Whitby. She's fell off the stage and broke her neck!' And she sat down again, hiding her face in her hands.

'She's come to no harm,' Mrs Potchard reassured her. 'Look, the note's in her own handwriting. She can't have broken her neck *and* written to tell you about it.'

She opened the folded paper and read aloud, her voice beginning to falter:

Dear Ma,
Just to let you know Cousin Gully and I are going on a quick jaunt with the Gen-u-ine Red Indians. I will take care of him and he will take care of me,

so we will both be safe and sound. I KNEW you
would understand. Bless you, dear Ma.

Your ever-loving daughter, Whitby Marvel.

Hetty gave a loud sob, and then turned on Leicester,
dry-eyed and furious. 'You knew about this, Leicester,
didn't you? You knew all along!'

'No, Ma, honest,' said poor Leicester, going even
pinker. 'A chap come just now from the theatre and give
me the letter. I never knew nuffing before it was read out.'

'He's telling the truth, Hetty. Don't take on so,' Mrs
Potchard said, to calm her down, although she was just
as furious herself. But she believed that Leicester would
never be able to keep a secret if he knew one. Nor was
he likely to let the other two go off without at least trying to go with them.

Hetty, now clutching *three* letters in her lap, wailed,
'All this readin' and writin', it don't do nobody any good!'

As they laid trays together at a side-table down the far
end of the kitchen, Clemency whispered to Poll, 'Who
are these for, anyway?'

'The master and mistress,' Poll replied. 'And don't look at me as you talk, or she'll come over here and bat us. You're not going to get me into trouble as well.'

Clemency glanced back over her shoulder at Mrs Curd, who was busy at the enormous cooking range.

'And don't look at *her*, neither!' Poll hissed. 'She's got eyes in the back of her head.'

'What are their names, the master and mistress?'

'Why, Mr Lestrange and Miss Lestrange. Don't you know nothin'?'

'No,' said Clemency. 'That's why I'm asking. I arrived from India just over a week ago, and I hardly know any-thing about England.'

'India!' breathed Poll. 'That's where they *eat* people, int it?'

'No,' said Clemency crossly. 'Only the tigers do that.'

'Tigers!' said Poll, and was stunned into silence.

'What are they like, the master and mistress?'

This time Poll broke her own rule and looked at Clemency. 'How should *I* know?' she asked. 'You don't think they drop in every afternoon for a bit of a chat, do you? Sit at the table and say: *How do, Poll, we come to pass the time of day, it's fearful dull upstairs! It's fearful dull down here*, I say. *Would you like to peel some spuds for us?*

Clemency had to try very hard not to laugh at this and the china cups rattled on her tray. Mrs Curd sensed that liberties were being taken and came over to put an end to it.

'Poll, put those trays in the hatch. Flea—over here!'

Clemency didn't like her new name, but she didn't dare protest.

During the evening, Mrs Curd shouted at her for not knowing where the fish knives were kept, then for dropping a clean dish-towel on the floor, and finally for daring to let out a squeak when she burnt her fingertips on a hot oven door. Clemency felt the strange mutinous sensation boiling up inside her again. She treats us like slaves, she thought. Our Indian servants at home were treated much better than I am now.

She strode up to Mrs Curd and said, 'I hadn't a bed or any covers last night. None of my belongings has arrived yet. I've nothing but what I stand up in. Do you *want* me to be dirty and cold?'

She could see Poll lurking behind an open cupboard door, and when Mrs Curd gave a hoot of contemptuous laughter, Poll made a terrible face. Clemency shook her head at the girl, as if to say, 'I can't stop now, even if it would be wiser to.'

'It's not my fault,' she continued. 'I didn't ask for any of this to happen. I ought to have some other clothes, and something to sleep on, and blankets. It's winter!'

'It's nothing to me if you're cold, but I can't have you going about looking filthy, not in my kitchen,' said Mrs Curd. 'In this house, maids have to buy their own uniforms.'

'Buy them?'

'From out of their first year's wages.'

First *year*, thought Clemency, I've barely been here a day yet.

'I'm not a maid. I've told you, I'm Clem—ow!'

Mrs Curd's huge finger and thumb pinched her by the ear and almost lifted Clemency from the ground. She thought her ear might be torn right off, but she managed to swallow the rest of her screech of pain.

Mrs Curd pushed her face up to Clemency's and her voice came out low and harsh. 'And *I've* told *you* to keep your trap shut. Do you want to go back in that larder—now, when it's pitch-dark, when it's night-time cold?'

Clemency tried to shake her head, though the sharp fingers still had her ear in their grip. She felt that a few more hours in the store cupboard would be little different from another cold night on the floor of Poll's dungeon, but she hated the thought of being locked in.

'I can't hear you.' The fingers pinched tighter.

'No,' Clemency whispered. 'I don't.'

Mrs Curd suddenly let her go, and she stood still, rubbing the life back into her sore ear.

Mrs Curd's mouth curled into a nasty little smile. 'I think we might be starting to learn,' she said, in a self-satisfied voice. 'As for blankets and such, that's the housekeeper's job, not mine.'

'Then I'll go and speak to the housekeeper about it,' said Clemency, even though Poll was waving at her frantically to stop.

The smile was wiped off Mrs Curd's face. 'You'll do no such thing, you rude young—!' She couldn't think of a word bad enough to describe Clemency and ended up by shouting, '—*creature*! You don't go nowhere, and you don't go speaking to no one, not if you know what's good for you.'

At the end of the long hard evening, as Clemency followed Poll and the quivering flame of the candle stump, she whispered, 'Do you know where things are kept in this house?'

'What things?' Poll whispered back, her pale face like a frightened ghost in the darkness of the corridor.

'Would you know, for instance, where the linen cupboards are?'

'No,' said Poll, looking stubborn. And then she wavered. 'But I know where the drying room is.'

'What's that?'

'Where they dry all the clothes and the sheets and stuff in the bad weather.'

'Show me.'

'What—now?'

Clemency nodded, and had to give Poll a quick push to get her moving. 'Yes, now. Now's the very best time.'

They set off again, down different passages and up and down steps. Poll found the drying room, and Clemency said, 'I bet they store the sheets and things nearby.' She took the candlestick from Poll and began to open and close doors along the corridor. Poll flattened herself to the wall as if trying to disappear, and whispered, 'Oh, Lor', Flea, do stop! Someone will hear you.'

Clemency found a huge cupboard stacked with neat piles of bed-linen, and next to it another with blankets and quilts. She put the candlestick carefully down on the floor and called to Poll, 'Come and take these.' She began flinging down blankets and sheets from the shelves she could reach.

'We can't, Flea. If they find us we'll be *killed*.'

'It's all my own stuff anyway,' Clemency said carelessly. 'If you look at it that way. My family's stuff.'

'I don't know what you're gabbin' on about. And they *will* find us.'

'No they won't.'

'They'll soon find that the stuff's gone.'

'Well, I don't care!' Clemency said, having run out of arguments. 'What else can they do to me?' She touched the tip of her ear, which was still sore. 'Lock me in larders, pinch me, shout in my face—well, I got through all that, didn't I?'

Poll looked down at the floor, mumbling, 'I don't know, but I wouldn't be so sure. People make fierce enemies in this house. They hold grudges and they don't never forget.'

Impatient, Clemency picked up a heap of bed-linen and thrust it into Poll's arms. She collected another heap herself, shut the cupboard doors and, carrying the candle, made her unhesitating way back down the twisting passages.

Despite her worries, Poll began to brighten up as they made themselves a warm nest on her mattress, smoothing out sheets and piling plump quilts on top of soft blankets.

'Ooh, aren't we something?' she said, giggling, rolling up a quilt and pushing it behind her head for a pillow.

Clemency noticed that the sheets were all embroidered with a white monogram—an intricately curled letter which she traced with her finger: $\mathcal{L}$.

'I suppose L is for Lestrange?' she said.

'Don't ask me. I don't know nothin' about these sheets, and I don't *want* to know nothin',' Poll replied. 'What I do know is that we must blow out this candle.'

'Oh, can't we stay awake a bit longer? I need to talk.'

'You can talk, but you must do it in the dark. I only gets given the candle ends and we must make this one last for the morning, or we shall never see what we're doing when we have to get up.'

'You might put on one of the sheets instead of your dress, and then you'd be for it!' Clemency laughed, but Poll shrunk away under the covers, softly muttering, 'Oh, Lor'.'

'We should have stolen some food as well,' Clemency went on, 'and brought that with us. I certainly know where the preserves are kept, but I couldn't get any open.'

'I bet I could've,' Poll said.

'My hands were too small.' Clemency spread out her fingers against the candlelight. Poll put out her hand too. Though overall she was as small and slight as Clemency, her hand was much bigger, the palm wide and strong.

'That comes of hard work,' Poll said, and then, with a quick movement, pinched out the candle-flame. They were in utter darkness, surrounded by the smell of waxy smoke.

'How old are you, Poll?'

'Thirteen.'

'And how long have you worked in the kitchen?'

'Since the spring.'

'How did you end up here?'

She felt Poll shrug in the dark. 'Vicar got me the job, didn't he? My big sis works at the vicarage. She's got it soft there, compared to me.'

'But why do you have to work? Couldn't you just stay at home with your mother and father?'

Poll let out a hard little laugh. 'What—all cosy together in the graveyard?'

'So you're an orphan then, like me,' Clemency said in wonder. She hadn't met any other orphans before.

'Yes, and it's better here than in the orphanage. At least, I think so . . .'

'Is that what would have happened to you otherwise?'

'That's where my little brothers are. And I ent seen them since they was took away.'

There was a long silence. Clemency felt Poll pull herself into a tight ball under the covers. But she continued to sit up, hugging her knees, her mind racing. Miss Clawe had delivered her straight to Mrs Curd; Mrs Curd had set her to work as a scullery maid; scullery maids, according to Poll, didn't last long. Is that what Miss Clawe wanted, for Clemency to disappear into the depths of this huge house and then disappear altogether? Why? And did her aunt even know that she had ever arrived? Did her aunt know about her existence at all?

Clemency shivered. She had plenty of warm covers tonight, but nothing could stop the chill feeling of dread that filled her stomach, and spread and spread.

Chapter 13
Red Indians

————○————

It was icy cold in the back of the Red Indians' wagon. Whitby had wrapped herself in a red zigzag-patterned blanket and managed somehow to sleep, but the chattering of his teeth kept Gully from falling into a doze, despite his exhaustion. His whole jaw seemed to be clacking together like a pair of loose nutcrackers. He didn't think he had ever been so cold. Or so cramped. His long limbs were folded into a tiny space in the back of the wagon, along with all the Indians' stage equipment and personal belongings and Whitby, who was squeezed in just behind the driver's box.

There were five Gen-u-ine Red Indians in the troupe. Two brothers, Fred and Alf, Fred's wife Josephine, and their nine-year-old son, Potter. Then there was Jerry, who was not related to the others but had joined them a year before and was now famous for his knife-throwing act. It was Jerry whom Whitby had her eye on.

Fred and Potter sat up on the driver's box of the wagon, while Jerry and Alf rode ahead on the two pie-bald horses that made up part of the act. Josephine had been left behind at her mother's in Brighton, where she had recently given birth to a baby girl. So the Red Indians were glad to have Whitby along. Even if she didn't know how to blow great plumes of fire from her mouth, she could fit into Josephine's costume and stand rock-still while knives were thrown at her. As for Gully, they hadn't found him a job so far. He felt they saw him as a great gangly boy who just got in the way.

A shout went up ahead, and the jolting wagon came to a halt. A cheerful face poked through the opening in the canvas flap. 'Breakfast stop!' it announced, on a stream of frosty air. 'Get up, you two, and stretch your legs.'

Outside the morning sky was a milky blue. Frost, and the smoky breath of the horses, and the sun all mingled together. Gully stretched and yawned. The horses snorted in a grumbling sort of way, then pricked up their ears as Potter appeared with their nosebags of oats. Alf was getting a small fire going, and Jerry scoured the ground for more firewood. Gully walked stiffly towards the fire and held his hands out to the flames. Alf cleared his throat a couple of times. Gully looked up to see Jerry signalling to him.

'You're not on holiday, you know,' he said in a low voice, when Gully went over to him. 'You've got to help out as much as everyone else. Very democratic, we Indians are. No bosses, no skivvies. Now, get picking up sticks, or there'll be no breakfast for you.'

Walking about and bending down got the blood flowing again round Gully's limbs. And then hot tea and bacon warmed him from the inside, too. Suddenly the cold morning on top of a hill in the middle of nowhere seemed much more appealing and his sense of adventure returned. There were just two small worries lurking at the back of his mind: one was that he would not be able to find Clemency, and the other was what his mother would say and do to him for running away with the Red Indians.

'So where is it you got to get to?' Alf asked, chewing through a thick crust and taking another swig of tea at the same time.

'Somewhere near Frome,' said Gully. 'It's a big house I'm looking for. I shall be able to ask where exactly it is when we get closer.'

'Just over in Somerset, then,' Fred said, and Alf said, 'Near Bristol, in't it?' and Fred replied, 'No, nearer Bath, I reckon.'

'After we've done Shaftesbury, then, and 'fore we get to Bath,' Alf pronounced.

Gully's heart sank. It would take for ever to get there.

'You'd do better,' Jerry said, his voice quick and bright in contrast to Alf and Fred's slow rhythms, 'to go straight from Salisbury to Warminster. Frome's about eight miles beyond.'

Alf chuckled. 'Listen to the boy! A right gee-ogg-rapher, he is.'

'Don't you remember where you picked me up last year?' Jerry asked them.

'Where you picked *us* up, more like, and took us for a ride,' Alf said, in a good-natured way.

'Taunton, was it? No, Tavistock. Something begin-ning with T,' said Fred.

'It was Trowbridge. I'd followed you all round after seeing you first at Bath. And at Trowbridge I threw the knife and split the walnut that you bet I couldn't split. And next day I packed up all my belongings and came on the road with you!'

Whitby listened to him in a glow of admiration.

'Well, it's a romantic tale an' all,' Alf muttered, 'but we've heard it before, an' besides, we was there.'

'I'm just reminding you that I come from that part of the country. That I wasn't born in a wagon with a feather in my bonnet!'

The brothers laughed at this, and Potter—who might well have been born like that, thought Gully—laughed the hardest.

'*We* weren't born so, neither, Little Hawk,' Alf said. 'In fact, if we were born anything, we were born the Three Singing Cavaliers, till our dear mama discovered that only big brother Bill had any talent in that direction. Us two was better at throwing things.' He leaned towards Whitby and explained, 'We come from a long line of Singing Cavaliers, my dear. Fred and I's only the first generation of Red Indians.'

'I quite understand,' Whitby replied. 'I myself was born to be sawn in half on stage, but sadly my pa died and my ma retired to take in lodgers. Dancing in the chorus was only a stop-gap till I could move on to something better.'

Alf looked at her with sympathy. 'I'd treat having knives thrown at you as a stop-gap, too.'

Fred doused the fire, and Potter went to remove the horses' nosebags. On the next leg of the journey,

Fred and Alf rode while Jerry drove the wagon. Gully perched beside him. The sun was well-risen and birds fluttered in the hedgerows. Warm again and well-fed, Gully began to see the pleasure in life on the open road.

'I know the countryside round Frome,' Jerry told him. 'I worked in a solicitor's office there before I chucked it all up to become a Red Indian. Where exactly do you want to get to?'

'The Great Hall, Caredew,' said Gully. 'That's all I've got to go on.'

Jerry screwed up his handsome features. 'The Great Hall, Caredew . . . I think I know it. It'll have to be after Shaftesbury and before Bath, but I can get you there,' he said cheerfully.

And just then, as they turned the corner of the hill, Salisbury lay before them in the sun, the spire of its cathedral pointing up into the sky like a ray of hope.

Chapter 14

The Kitchen Garden

——○——

There was a different feeling in the air the next morning. Brilliant winter sunshine poured in through the tall kitchen windows, turning the vast scrubbed tabletop white as a seashell, and glinting off the rows of copper pans. It made Clemency feel almost cheerful. It must have had the same effect on Mrs Curd, for she was actually humming as she worked.

Poll wasn't cheerful, though. She came rushing through to the scullery with a stack of dishes, looking like an angry bull was chasing her. She set them down on the draining-board and began carefully spooning cooked meat from a pan into the dishes. Even when each was full she wasn't satisfied, and poked the slivers of meat with a finger, swapping some around and rearranging others.

Clemency peered over her shoulder. 'Who are those for?'

Poll picked up one of the dishes. It had pictures of small furry dogs all round the outside.

'For *dogs*?' asked Clemency, incredulous.

'The mistress's dogs. And I'm late. And the bowls must be all the same, and the meat must look nice and tasty.'

It does, thought Clemency. It looked nicer and tastier than some of the meat that was served in Aunt Hett's kitchen.

'Why do they get such special treatment? They're only dogs.'

Poll shook her head. 'Not these ones. It's like they're her children. Not just ordinary children, neither—little princes and princesses.'

'So they dine out of china bowls, and they eat the best meat?'

'And for all I know they got tables and chairs. I never bin up there to see. I just have to put their meals out, and get them perfect every time or I'm in dead trouble.'

'How many dogs has she got?'

Poll picked up four bowls, two in each hand, and jerked her head towards the others. 'You can count, can't you? Bring them two, quick as you can.'

Clemency followed her towards the little service lift they sent the trays up in. Poll set the bowls inside with great care, prodding again at the slices of meat to make them look their best. She muttered, 'They say she loves those dogs so much she's going to leave them all her money when she dies. And then Miss Clawe will be in clover.'

'Why?'

Poll shut the lift door and began to work at the pulleys.

'Why? Because a dog can't spend its own sovereigns, can it? A dog can't order up a dinner, or send for the carriage. It needs a person to do that. And that person will be Miss Clawe.'

Clemency stood motionless, her mind digesting these new facts. But Poll had already turned away, and with a gloomy stare surveyed the mound of washing-up still to be done. 'Better get on with this before old mother Curd sees us with our hands empty.'

And she went off to fetch hot water.

When she came back, and they had filled the sink, Clemency said, 'Tell me more about the household.'

Poll shook her head. 'Nothin' more to tell.'

'You must know more if you've been here since last spring.'

'I don't want to know,' Poll said. 'I keep my head down. If I behave myself and do my job right I might get moved up from scullery maid to somethin' better.' And then she thought of the stolen sheets and blankets and felt sick.

In silence Clemency rinsed a plate and lifted it on to the rack to drain. It was made of gleaming white porcelain with a gold design all round the rim, loops of elegant capital *L*s. The Lestranges even had their initial on the china.

'What I *do* know,' Poll whispered, 'is that the mister and missus is like two armies fightin' each other. An' they expect all the servants to line up with 'em, one side or the other.'

'Which side are you on?'

Poll looked at her as though she was stupid. 'Mrs Curd's, of course. And so are you. Got no choice.'

'And whose side is *she* on?'

Poll pursed her lips and went on stubbornly wiping the same plate round and round, as if she would scrub away the design. But she said no more.

Clemency was standing at the big table grating sugar from the cone when a new face appeared at the kitchen door.

'Oh, Mr Ermine,' Mrs Curd said, putting down her spoon and wiping her hands. 'About time.'

'Hard frost this morning, Mrs Curd. Can't do nothing fast with a hard frost,' the old man replied, unmoved by her sharp tone.

He had brought the day's produce for the cook to inspect. Clemency, busy behind the tall cone of sugar, was able to watch him without attracting Mrs Curd's attention. He was a small man with a weather-beaten face. His jacket and waistcoat were a colour Clemency could only think of as *manure*, probably most practical in his job, since he was the gardener. She must have been locked in the larder when he came the day before. The two of them went through the basket, Mrs Curd complaining about the quality of the sprouts and Mr Ermine defending his vegetables.

'There's grapes for Mr Theo, and a peach for Miss Honoria. And a rosebud for each of 'em, though who'll have the red and who'll have the white, they can fight it out atween 'em. Fought like cats all their lives, that pair. Ent none of my business, thank the Lord.'

'Nor mine neither,' sighed Mrs Curd. 'But don't let Miss Clawe hear you talk like that, or you'll be for it.'

'I'll be for it, I'll be for it,' the old man muttered. 'I never go near Miss Clawe, so there's no danger of that.'

The basket empty now, he pulled his cap back on and made to leave, still mumbling under his breath.

'A drop of tea, Mr Ermine?' Mrs Curd said, waiting until the last moment before offering.

'No, thank you, missus,' he replied. 'I'm off to the Little Hall now. I'll get one there.' And he stomped away, with the bow-legged walk of an old jockey. As he went, Clemency heard him mumble, 'An' a warmer welcome, too, from dear old Molly Diamond.'

This conversation was as good as a feast to Clemency. As she went about her tasks her mind was busy with all the facts she had picked up. Miss Honoria and Miss Lestrange had to be one and the same person, and Mr Theo must be Mr Lestrange: the master and mistress. And they fought over silly things like the colour of the rosebuds sent up by the gardener. Miss Honoria must be her aunt. Then was Mr Theo her uncle? If so, he must be the Master at the Great Hall. Ermine, who seemed far more talkative than anyone Clemency had so far encountered, was likely to know a great deal more.

Later that morning, while helping Mrs Curd, she dropped in a casual question. 'Has Mr Ermine been with the family a long time?'

'A long time? I'll say. For ever, more like.'

Mrs Curd stepped back to open the oven door, brushed against the table, and knocked a colander of sprouts on to the floor.

'Mercy me! Get under there and pick them all up, girl,' she said, thrusting Clemency under the table, and giving her a push with her boot for good measure. 'That's what comes of nosy questions!' she added.

Clemency gathered up the sprouts, then crawled out from under the table, holding a peach. 'What about this?'

Mrs Curd snatched it and examined it: one side was squashed to pulp where it hit the stone floor.

'Lord, that will never do. Run out to Ermine and see if you can get another. Miss H. will have me flayed if I can't send up a peach for her dinner. You'll find him in the bothy, this weather, over the fire, or in the stove-house pretending to work. Don't bother looking outside, it's much too cold for him.'

Clemency ran, before Mrs Curd had time to change her mind or decide that the bruised peach was her fault.

The amazing thing was that she hadn't lost her temper over it.

Clemency had not been outside for two whole days, and the fresh air was intoxicating. She took off across the yard as fast as she could run. Ahead and to her right were only outbuildings, but to her left there was a long wall of honey-coloured stone with a wooden gate set in it. On the other side she glimpsed a different world from the bare paved yard. She had never been in a real English garden before, let alone an English kitchen garden. Within the high walls, she found a chequerboard of cultivated beds and neat paths, all sparkling with frost. Against the far wall stood a row of glasshouses, their windows reflecting the sun. It was the first beautiful sight she had seen since arriving in England.

There was also a little cottage built into one corner— it almost looked like something growing out of the walls. Smoke rose from the cottage chimney, so Clemency started towards it, mindful of what Mrs Curd had said. But before she got there she heard a voice calling from one of the glasshouses.

'What can I do for you, then?'

Mr Ermine leaned in the doorway, puffing on a pipe.

'Mrs Curd sent me to ask if there was another ripe peach. Please,' she added.

Without a word, Mr Ermine turned away. Unsure if he meant her to, Clemency followed him.

He made his way through the tunnel-like glasshouse. Pots of ferns lined the pathway. Overhead, grapes hung from ancient vines. There was a strange smell, earthy and damp, but it was nothing like the ripe smells of Indian vegetation. Mr Ermine came to a sudden stop in a small room with a table and a tap and an old wooden chair. He picked up the stem of a plant and started pulling off the dead leaves, as if this was the job he'd been doing before Clemency interrupted.

'Who are you, then?' he asked.

'I work in the kitchen.'

'Not seen you afore.'

Clemency decided not to mention who she really was just yet. It hadn't got her anywhere with Mrs Curd, and Mr Ermine might be just as bad. 'I'm new,' she said.

He turned to her and gave her a shrewd, squinting look. 'Like a look round, would you? We don't get many visitors here.'

'Yes, please, if you can spare the time.'

150

'Can't do you a peach, though. What's Mrs Curd want two for?' he asked, leading the way again, opening a door into a sweltering section of glasshouse where exuberant flowers bloomed orange and crimson and purple. This is more like India, Clemency thought.

'She knocked the other one on the floor and squashed it.'

To her surprise, Mr Ermine laughed. 'And now she wants another one to cover up her mistake? Well, she's out o' luck.'

He stopped to pull down a flower and sniff it, then held the stem lower for Clemency to smell, too.

'It's the devil's job to keep folks up at the big house in fancy fruit and flowers all year round. Don't want nothin' when it's in season, only when it's darned awkward to grow. I've got one more peach but it ent ripe yet. She can have it if she wants to give Miss H. the belly-ache. That's all it's fit for at present.'

Beyond the next door, the air was cooler.

Mr Ermine went on, 'Why they can't be satisfied with good keeping apples and pears in winter, and straw-berries and peaches as the season comes around, like ordinary folk, I can't fathom. Specially since we don't have the extra help when we need it. Do we, young Jem?'

As he called out, Clemency noticed a figure in a patch of sunlight, working away at a pile of straw. For a moment she thought that Mr Ermine was joking when he called him *young* Jem, for he had a shock of white hair. But the face that looked up and gave her a shy smile was that of a boy, and she saw that his eyebrows and eyelashes were white too, and his eyes very pale. As he bent over the straw, which the sunlight spun into gold, she thought of Rumplestiltskin.

'Young Jem's my reg'lar help. He's not too bright, but he's good at the really useful jobs, digging, and washing the pots, an' that. And making the straw shields for the tender shrubs, like he's doing now. But we're a bit behind this season, ent we, Jem? That job should've been done a long time ago. You can't rely on the help when you need it these days, so it seems. Men sent off here and there, gaddin' about the country, all on the mistress's say-so. Never there when you want 'em. When you need 'em. So it's all left to me and Jem.'

He saluted Jem with a wave of his pipe. Jem smiled back but said nothing.

Mr Ermine carried on, 'Yet they still wants a peach any day of the year they fancy, as if they was picking it off one o' the tapestries on the dining-room wall. Oh, they're as mad as pilchards up there at the big house.'

'Mad?' asked Clemency.

'Insane. Stark raving sideways. That's my opinion. I don't care who hears me. No one comes out 'ere to visit us anyways. No one *does* hear me.'

Mr Ermine set off, retracing his steps through the glasshouses. Trotting after him, Clemency tried again. 'Why do you say mad?'

'Would you call it normal human behaviour not to speak to your brother for twenty-five years? Your own brother what lives not a hundred steps away down the corridor? Or not to set eyes on a sister for twenty-five years, given she lives in the same house?'

'Is that really what they're like?'

'Madness,' said Mr Ermine, sighing. He pointed his pipe-stem at Clemency. 'And they've taken the whole crew down with them. All mad, up at the Great Hall. You watch yourself, missy. They'll get you, one way or the other. We're best out of it, me and Jem, out here on our own. Jem might be simple, but he's a darned sight more sensible than them.'

He paused, breathing loudly. Clemency hoped he wasn't mad too. His face had turned a deep shade of red while he'd been ranting on.

'What shall I say about the peach?' she asked.

'Oh, the peach. Well, I can't magic up another one for her, I ent no conjurer, though I do manage some fine tricks. Here's one. Offer her this instead to take her mind off it. Miss H. will like this. The first camellia flower of winter.' And he snipped a beautiful pale pink blossom, like a perfect unfurling rose, from a tall shrub with dark green leaves.

'It looks just like tea,' said Clemency, stroking a shiny leaf.

'What's that?'

'Like tea. I don't mean in a teapot. I mean when it's growing in tea plantations.'

Mr Ermine frowned. 'Very likely, missy. Camellias is in the same family—like cousins—talking from a plant's point of view. Not that I ever saw a tea plant, meself.'

They reached the place where he had his work bench, and Mr Ermine paused to wire a couple of leaves behind the camellia flower to make a pretty button-hole. 'All behind-hand this season,' he sighed, gesturing with his pipe at the pile of old newspapers and the pots of geraniums waiting to be wrapped up and put into store for winter. 'Can't make no sense of all this gaddin' about.'

He showed her to the door. Clemency shivered in the cold outside air.

'Run back, missy, before you catch your death. I've probably kept you much too long. Blame it on me when you see Mrs Curd. Blame me, everyone always does.'

He gazed after Clemency thoughtfully as she picked a path across the garden to the gate in the wall.

'Well, I never. Now, where did I put that old copy of *The Times*?' he murmured, but she was too far away to hear.

Chapter 15
Truly a Marvel

——++○++——

Mrs Potchard sat in Troy Porter's parlour thawing her frozen hands. She slipped her toes under the warm furry side of one of the snoozing spaniels. The journey from Southampton had been long and cold.

Aunt Troy was reading the papers she had brought, the two letters to Lucie Wrigglesworth and the note from Whitby. When she finished she peered at her sister over the top of her spectacles, giving her one of the special looks she reserved for pupils at her school who were trying to be bad. The look said: *You can't surprise me. Whatever you do, I've seen it all, I've heard it all, before.*

'What do you think?' Mrs Potchard asked.

'It hardly looks good, does it, sister?'

'What should I do?'

'Precisely what you've meant to do all along, ever since you read the note from Miss Whitby.' She pronounced Whitby's name very clearly and precisely, to show how much she disapproved of that young lady. 'Go to Somerset, and rescue them all from certain disaster.'

Mrs Potchard smiled in relief.

'And I would advise you to see a lawyer on the way. Perhaps one in Somerset, who could give you local information.'

'I hadn't thought of that,' Mrs Potchard said. 'First I have just one small errand to get out of the way. I have to take a Miss Boniface to Hertfordshire to visit her ailing grandfather. Not that her presence will make him feel any better!'

'You shouldn't make light of such things, Dolly,' Troy said. 'Besides, why can't her nursemaid, or companion, or *someone*, do the fetching and carrying?'

'If they did, I would be out of a job,' Mrs Potchard replied. 'Besides, the money will pay for me to get to Somerset and back, and more.'

'You mustn't worry about that, Dolly,' Troy told her. 'I have an interest in seeing that my esteemed nephew Gulliver doesn't come to mischief. And Whitby, too, I suppose,' she added. 'I will give you the money for your trip.'

Mrs Potchard's cheeks glowed red. 'I can't let you do that.'

'But you must.'

They were still arguing politely when Ellen came in with the tea tray and told them sharply to stop.

The two piebald horses, Betty and Brownie, were transformed. Brightly coloured saddle cloths, feathers plaited in their manes, and a lick of greasepaint round the eyes gave them a warrior-like appearance. Gully, who held their bridles, felt dull by comparison in his old brown suit.

On stage, Running Rain, Medicine Man, Little Hawk and Two Bears, in fringed costumes and beads and feathers, beat upon skin drums, danced in a circle, and turned dizzying somersaults. Medicine Man wore an alarming head-dress like an animal skull complete with horns. He cast powders into a bowl of fire, sending up thick clouds of purple smoke, out of which stepped Whitby, dressed in the costume Josephine had once worn. Her black hair was parted in the middle and plaited beneath a headband of turquoise beads. She certainly looked the part. Aunt Hett might have said that it wasn't in her blood to be a Red Indian, but surely she would have been thrilled to see Whitby stepping proudly through the smoke just like an Indian princess. She strode in front of a wooden screen, emblazoned with strange symbols, while Little Hawk danced on, whirling tomahawks, two in each hand.

Gully bit his lower lip. Being sawn in half was nothing compared to this. There was no risk in being sawn in half, except the risk of the cabinet falling apart and revealing its trick to the audience. But Jerry held real tomahawks, and he was really going to fling them, and it was Whitby, not Josephine, who stood waiting in front of the target.

Two Bears rolled out a thunder of anticipation on the drums. Whitby held out her arms stiffly, raised to shoulder height at each side. Jerry whirled the tomahawks once more, then threw, one from his left hand and one from his right. Gully shut his eyes, but that couldn't stop him hearing the thuds as the tomahawks landed.

The audience gasped. He opened one eye.

Whitby was smiling, her teeth brilliant white against her brown stage make-up. A tomahawk stuck out of each armpit. Jerry whirled again, dropping the remaining two tomahawks low and almost skipping over them as he danced. Then—whistle, thud—the first one over her right shoulder, the second over her left. Gully kept his eyes open this time. He breathed a sigh of relief that the ordeal was over.

Jerry grinned at the audience, and bowed. As he bent low he removed a knife from a sheath strapped to his leg. The audience gasped again. He held up the gleaming blade so that it flashed in the stage lights, looking even bigger and sharper and more wicked than it really was. Even Whitby looked shaken. She shrunk her body down, making herself as small against the target as she could. But the tomahawks beneath her arms stopped her from moving very far. The glittering blade flew from Jerry's hand, embedding itself with a thwack barely an inch above her head. The audience let out their breath and burst into applause.

Medicine Man sent up a cloud of mustard-coloured smoke which allowed Whitby to wriggle out from between the blades, and run off into the wings.

'Are you all right?' Gully asked, as he handed the horses over to Two Bears for the finale.

'Look at me!' Whitby held out a shaking hand. But she was smiling fit to burst her face. 'Wasn't he amazing? I must've stretched up six inches when the first ones came at me, and shrunk six inches for the second lot. I nearly died of fright.'

'Well, sit down a minute and recover,' Gully recommended.

'No. I must take my bow!'

Whitby rushed back on stage. One of the Indians swept her up behind him, on to Betty or Brownie in disguise, and all five of them made Indian farewells and left in a cloud of dust.

'Get them 'orses out of 'ere, right away,' said the stage manager, untouched by the waves of applause still battering the auditorium. 'Used to think dogs was bad enough in a theatre, but 'orses! 'Orses is worst of all!' And he clucked his tongue and shooed at Gully and the Indians, as a comic in a loud green suit rushed past them on to the stage.

'No,' said Jerry, politely. 'Seals are the worst. *Much* worse than horses. You wait till you've had seals here. Think of all that water.'

But the stage manager didn't care to be disagreed with, and made louder and grumpier noises until they were outside in the yard.

'What we really want,' said Alf, removing his animal skull and shaking his head vigorously, then poking a finger in his ear, 'what we really need—is our own tent.'

'In summer we do fields and fairgrounds,' Fred explained to Gully. 'You don't get stage managers or nobody complaining about the horses then.'

'The horses are an essential part of the act,' said young Potter. He tried to stop a yawn, then opened his mouth so wide to let it out that his feather head-dress popped right off the back of his head.

'Whitby was very good,' said Gully, who felt his cousin's bravery and professionalism had been rather ignored in the last few minutes.

'Yes, not bad, not bad,' mused Alf, and Fred added, 'Pity that she can't breathe fire, though, like my Josephine.'

'She was a *marvel*,' said Jerry, grinning a wide white grin. 'Truly, a marvel.'

After the talk with her sister Dolly, Troy Porter passed a restless night, full of odd dreams—which was most unlike her. She recalled Gully's visit, and her promise to keep her eyes and ears open for him. She hadn't kept that promise, again most unlike her. So, once morning lessons were underway, she put on her hat and set out up Squat's Lane towards the square at the end.

It was a day of freezing fog. She couldn't see across the road, and it took her a while to grope her way to Watkyn's sweetshop. She opened the door and the bell clanged softly. No one appeared. From beyond a curtained-off doorway at the back of the shop, Miss Porter could hear voices. She examined a tray of pink sugar mice, their eyes dots of white icing and their neat tails made of string. The sweetshop was strictly forbidden to the girls in her school, and Miss Porter had never been inside, and yet these sugar mice seemed strangely familiar. Only last week she had confiscated one just like this from a girl who was secretly nibbling away at it in the back of her history class.

She turned her attention to a heap of gleaming liquorice comfits. Still nobody came. One of the voices behind the curtain—a child's—rose in complaint. A man replied, gently, 'No, out of the question. Can't have that fog getting on your chest. You've a most important day tomorrow, and you must be well for that. Why don't you read a book?'

The child grumbled again. 'I've read every book in the house, and—*I am bored*!'

Being bored—and complaining about it—was also strictly forbidden in Miss Porter's school, but she couldn't help feeling just a little bit sorry for this child. The voices went on.

'Have you replied to the latest letter? You must make a good impression, you know.'

'Mother and I posted it yesterday. D'you think I'd fall behind with my valuable scientific correspondence?'

Miss Porter coughed into her hand.

They must have heard her, for a balding little man swept the curtain aside and stepped into the shop. He was shaped like a pouter pigeon, in a silvery-fronted waistcoat, with an apron tied round his substantial middle. 'Good morning, Madam—not that it's a very good morning outdoors. What can I do for you?'

'Good morning. Mr Watkyn, is it?'

The stout man puffed his front out even more. Miss Porter expected to hear him burble like a pigeon. Instead he said, 'Indeed it is. Mr Watkyn of Watkyn's High Class Confectionery.'

He was obviously a vain man. Miss Porter hoped that she could make use of this. She put one finger to her chin and said, 'Ah, now, I wonder if you *can* help me. Just the other day someone was telling me about a confectioner's shop in this neighbourhood.'

Mr Watkyn rose on his toes and leaned forward. 'Something good, I hope?'

'Let me see . . .' Out of the corner of her eye she noticed that the curtain had opened a fraction and the pale moon-face of a young boy was peering out. He looked rather sullen. 'Yes, a friend of mine who travels a great deal ran into someone with a most intriguing name. Now, can I recall what it was? Lancaster? No, that's not memorable enough. Lymanster?'

Mr Watkyn continued to wobble on tiptoe, his eyebrows raised in anticipation, but said nothing.

'Ah, I remember now,' Miss Porter went on. 'The name was Lysander. And conversation came round to London, somehow, and to this part of London, and the person called Lymanster—'

'Lysander,' the boy corrected her.

Miss Porter turned and gave him what she hoped was a friendly smile. From inside it felt rather crocodilian. 'Lysander. Thank you. How clever you are. This person mentioned a connection of theirs who was something to do with a—a sweetshop. A confectioner's of *very* good reputation. But I understand that this place is called Watkyn's.' She let her mouth droop a little.

'It is,' said Mr Watkyn, with some pride.

'Not Lysander's? Then do you know where I might find a shop of that name?'

'No. I really can't imagine what—'

'They must have meant Mother,' said the boy. He pushed aside the rest of the curtain. His plump face was matched with a tubby body stuffed into a velvet suit. He wore a tight Eton collar which turned his double chin into a treble chin. 'Mother's name was Lysander before she married. And had me,' he added, with some satisfaction.

'My, my,' said Miss Porter.

'Then they *were* talking about this shop,' said his father. 'Of course, there's nothing else in this part of London to match our—'

'*Who* was mentioning Mother's name?' the boy interrupted.

Miss Porter didn't like the sharp look in his eye.

'Tush tush, Bertie! How do we speak to customers?' Mr Watkyn reached out to put a stop to such bad manners, but ended by fondly dusting the boy's head with the flat of his hand.

'I don't speak to customers,' Bertie answered back, and then to Miss Porter he announced, 'I don't serve in the shop. I have more important things to do.'

'My, my,' said Miss Porter again.

'So pray, do tell, who was it that mentioned Mother's name?'

'Oh . . .' Miss Porter tried to sound as vague as possible. 'A friend who falls into conversation with all sorts of people on their travels to far-off places.'

'Such as?' demanded the boy.

Mr Watkyn laughed indulgently. 'He's very inquisitive, my boy. His mother and I can't keep up with the speed of his brain. Just a sponge for knowledge, soaks it up wherever he can find it.'

'I'm pleased to hear that,' said Miss Porter, who really was. But she didn't want Bertie's lightning brain at work on her own enquiries. She frowned and murmured, 'Mmm, this friend of mine has travelled to Africa and India. They have even been as far as China. I'm afraid I don't recall *where* they said they ran into the person called Lysander.'

'I didn't know our reputation stretched so far!' Mr Watkyn laughed.

The boy gave him an impatient look. 'Only it *is* rather strange,' he persisted. 'So far as we know, Mother hasn't got any relations in far-flung parts. Only Uncle, down in Somerset.'

Miss Porter cocked her head at this, only to find Bertie's gleaming eye fixed on her. She turned away quickly and pointed at the sugar mice. 'How much for the whole tray?' she enquired.

Stepping into her kitchen, Miss Porter brought a swirl of dirty fog in with her. Ellen was just sliding a vast pan of rice pudding into the oven.

'Ellen, do you know Mrs Watkyn, of Watkyn's Confectioners?'

'Only well enough to nod good morning, Miss P. Why do you ask?'

'It may be nothing . . . just some silliness of my nephew's. Apparently her maiden name was Lysander, and the family have connections in Somerset.'

Ellen began wiping crumbs off the table, talking as she worked. 'I don't know about that. Just what I see up and down the street. The Watkyns with their son, Bertie. Never goes out on his own, that child, always got his ma or pa with him.'

'They say he's very bright.'

Ellen chuckled. 'He looks like a piglet in a suit.'

'He's a cunning piglet, then.'

'They think the world of their boy, I know that much. They'd do anything for him.'

Miss Porter said, half to herself, 'Making myself sound a fool—so undignified—and I still don't know what it has to do with Gulliver's little friend. If it has any connection at all.'

Ellen pointed at the package under her employer's arm. 'What have you got there, Miss P.?'

Miss Porter sighed. 'Three dozen sugar mice,' she said.

'Whatever for?'

'Hmm.' Miss Porter frowned. 'I think I've broken one of my own rules.'

Chapter 16
Crime and Punishment

──┼┼○┼┼──

That night Clemency lay warm in the stolen covers. There had been no mention of them all day and she was beginning to think that she really had got away with it. On the floor stood a jar of peaches, which it had taken Poll only seconds to unscrew. They feasted on this sticky treat by the light of a whole candle Clemency had taken from one of the kitchen drawers, where it was kept for waxing the drawer runners to keep them opening smoothly. Poll, who ate most of the peaches, said at each mouthful that she wasn't able to enjoy them one bit, knowing that they would both be killed as soon as Mrs Curd noticed a jar was missing.

'It was such a job to filch the spare key and slip out and steal these peaches,' Clemency said. 'I wish they'd made me a housemaid instead of a scullery maid. I could get about so much more as a housemaid.'

She sat back, full to bursting, thinking what a good thief she made, and how Gully would be proud of her sleight-of-hand. And how even Whitby might be impressed at her audacity. Thinking about them kept her mind from darker places, until she fell asleep.

Next morning, after breakfast, Mrs Curd sent her to collect the dishes from the servants' hall. Two housemaids, a lady's maid, and an elderly manservant with a stooped back were finishing off their meal. When Clemency entered they fell silent. They were all neatly dressed in clean, well-pressed outfits. Clemency felt a shabby fright in her stained blue frock. Her maid's cap and apron, though clean, were miles too big. The two housemaids looked at each other and burst into giggles.

'May I clear the table now?' Clemency asked.

She was just reaching for the first dirty plate when the door to the corridor was wrenched open. Miss Clawe, tall, and black as a raven, loomed in the doorway. Everyone froze. She fixed her beady eye on Clemency, and the rest of the room let out the tiniest sigh of relief. But they flinched again when Miss Clawe gave a furious hiss.

'What is the meaning of *this*!'

She held up a pillowcase, dangling it from her black-net-covered fingers.

'It—it's a pillowcase,' Clemency said. She heard the other servants suck in their breath.

'It is a pillowcase, *Miss Clawe*,' Miss Clawe muttered between clenched teeth.

Then she grabbed Clemency by the wrist, twisted it upwards, and forced her outside. She pushed her down the corridor, round all the twists and turns which Clemency had come to know in the last few days, until they were in the dingy passageway outside Poll's room. The door stood open, and a weeping Poll crouched inside, guarded by a footman. On the floor, beside the heap of bed linen, was the sticky, empty jar.

'And what have you got to say about this!' Miss Clawe spat out the words.

'Oh, Flea,' Poll sobbed, her thin shoulders heaving under her apron straps.

Clemency felt the devil stirring in her again, just as when she'd answered back to Mrs Curd. She straightened her shoulders, stood as tall as she could manage (which was not very big at all), and hoped she could hold her nerve.

'I have got something to say. I *have*. If she's complaining that I didn't share them with her, she's right!' And she jabbed a finger at Poll.

Poll looked up, her tear-blotched face blank with confusion.

Clemency went on, gathering confidence. 'She wouldn't share with me that first night I was here, and I nearly froze to death. She's been really mean to me, so when I took the sheets and eiderdowns I wouldn't let her have any. And I ate the peaches right in front of her, just to spite her!'

Miss Clawe looked at Poll, who was beginning to understand what Clemency was up to, and said, 'Is that correct?'

Poll nodded mutely. Miss Clawe signed to the footman to take her away.

'Back to the kitchen with that one. She'll be more use there than shut up in some cupboard doing nothing.' She turned back to Clemency and flicked her hand at the muddle of sheets on the floor. 'As for you! Pick up all these—these *items*. First, they'll have to be washed, and you can do it all yourself. Then I shall decide what your punishment will be.'

And she turned away, expecting Clemency to follow her.

—————H—o—H—————

Clemency gazed about the bleak laundry. There were a number of stone sinks around the walls, and a huge copper for boiling water, unlit, in one corner. The floor sloped to a drain in the centre. Outside was an enclosed yard, with moss on the walls and empty clothes-lines. Not a single beam of sunshine found its way in.

'You'll stay here till they're done,' Miss Clawe instructed her. 'There's no hot water. Have to be cold. And I want them spotless—spotless, you hear!'

The two housemaids lurked just outside the door, their hands full of brooms and dusters. To them Miss Clawe said, 'Mary, Nancy, you'll take turns to keep an eye on her. And Mary—dog hairs on the sofas in the Blue Room. Nancy—the main staircase. I will be checking your work later.'

With that, her heels clicked briskly away down the corridor.

Both maids must still have been outside, for Clemency heard one say, 'Dog hairs, always dog hairs! Miss H.

should train those blasted dogs to clean up after themselves, since she's convinced they're so clever. Nasty creatures—one of them nipped me on the ankle when I was doing the fireplace.'

The other replied, 'If she thinks we can be in two places at once, *she* should try it. I can't get the whole staircase done in time if I'm stuck here.'

One of the maids poked her head round the laundry door. 'You stay right there, you scrawny little rat. I don't know what you've done, but I'm sure you deserve it!'

The other maid joined her. They both stared at Clemency, their eyes hard. She rolled up her sleeves and plunged her hands into one of the sinks.

'And keep at it,' the second one warned. 'I'm not getting into trouble just because of you. Don't move an inch. We'll be back before you know it.'

And they went off, whispering and giggling, their brushes and dustpans clanking. She could hardly believe they'd left her alone. If she was going to get out of Miss Clawe's clutches, now might be her only chance.

She took her hands out of the empty sink and looked around. A connecting door opened into an ironing room. There were stacks of maids' dresses and frilled aprons, starched and ironed, waiting on a table.

She chose the smallest she could find and quickly put them on. She knotted up her hair, then fitted on a maid's cap, much neater than her kitchen bonnet. She couldn't leave her own dirty frock to be found so rolled it up into a bundle. There were other clothes in the room—men's outdoor clothes, not uniforms—but they all seemed too large to be of use. Nevertheless, she snatched up a few, added them to her bundle, and ran out into the corridor with it. There was no one in sight. Heart banging inside her ribs, keeping her head down, she hurried along.

She was going to look for her aunt. Miss Clawe might try to keep her hidden away in the servants' quarters, but Clemency was going anyway, to find out what her aunt had to say about it.

In the countryside, there was a scattering of snow on the bone-hard fields and the sky looked leaden, as if there was more to come. Gully and Jerry, whose turn it was to ride at the back of the wagon, wrapped themselves in blankets and let their feet dangle, bumping against the tailboard.

'This is the life!' said Jerry.

'Is it?' asked Gully dubiously. He was thinking of Aunt Hett's cosy kitchen, of clean woollen socks knitted by his mother and warmed on the range before he put them on in the morning. Of Hetty's fruit tarts, straight from the oven, so hot they burnt your mouth. He even thought of his bed in the attic, long enough for him to stretch right out in.

'We're a week at Bath,' Jerry said, noticing his gloomy tone. 'We'll have rooms there. You can get a good night's sleep.'

'I shan't be going as far as Bath,' Gully reminded him. 'I haven't come on this jaunt for my own sake, and nor has Whitby. She's determined to get her ma's money back somehow. So I don't know what you'll do for target practice then.'

They both fell silent, thinking their own thoughts. The wagon jolted along, finding every rut and pothole, and the road unwound behind them, empty and still.

Eventually Gully asked, 'Have you been back in these parts since you ran away? Does your family know you're coming?'

'There's only my father. I send him a picture-post-card every now and then, show him where I've been and tell him where I'm going. I doubt he'll come and see the show, though. He's a sober sort, all work and no play.'

'Tell me about this Great Hall place, then. What do you know about it?'

Jerry said, 'A house in a large park, if I remember right. I often went on calls to the big houses with my father, and waited for him in the gig while he conducted business inside. Sometimes a maid would come out with some cake for me, and the groom would hold our horse and gossip or tell jokes.'

'They did that at the Great Hall?' Gully said eagerly, thinking that this sounded better than he had anticipated.

'No, not there. It was a great gloomy place, I seem to recall. Never got any treats there. Now at Dalton the surgeon's, his wife always gave me mince pies. Always seemed to have mince pies, whatever the time of year.'

'What about the family at the Great Hall, can you remember anything about them?'

Jerry thought hard, twisting his handsome features into a variety of expressions. 'Nope. No, I don't think I do. And my father never was much for talking—he'd call it *idle chatter.*'

'They had an odd name. Lestrange. Whitby over-heard this woman, Miss Clawe.'

'Clawe? Well, that's a name I know. Plenty of Clawes in those parts.'

'Miss Clawe's the housekeeper. At least, that's what Whitby heard her say.'

'Don't you believe this Miss Clawe?'

'I wasn't there to see her, but I don't trust anyone in the whole set-up. It reeks to high heaven of something bad.'

Jerry pondered on this. Then he said, in his usual optimistic way, 'Well, Shaftesbury's next, and then we're on our way! You'll soon find out what's up.'

But Gully, who could only see the rust-brown land stretching out behind him, and the iron-grey sky heavy with snow, and whose feet were so cold they had no sensation in them at all, felt very low. Very low indeed.

Chapter 17
Aunt

——o——

Clemency knew her way around much of the servants' areas by now, but the *above stairs* parts of the house were a complete mystery to her. Ahead was an important-looking door lined with green baize which looked likely. If she didn't try it she'd never find out.

She pushed it open cautiously and found herself in a huge hallway, very wide and high and full of light. A marble floor swept away in front of her, dotted here and there with towering potted palms and enormous vases of oriental design. There was no one in sight. She slipped out of the doorway and dodged as far as a little oasis formed by three pots of palms and a waist-high blue-and-white china jar with a lid in the shape of a pineapple. She had to hide her bundle of clothes so she stuffed them into the jar and carefully replaced the lid.

There was a scratching noise coming from somewhere, distant but regular. Peering through the palm
leaves, she spotted the white apron-bow of a housemaid, on her knees, brushing the stairs, step by step. It
must be the one called Nancy.

The stairs were a magnificent double flight, two
matching staircases rising from the floor to meet briefly
at a landing halfway up and spring apart again before
reaching the upper floor. Luckily for Clemency, the maid
was working on the flight furthest away. She slipped out
from her hiding place and dodged up the nearest stairs
to the halfway landing. There she paused, crouching behind the ornately carved banisters. The sweeping sound
continued safely below.

She ran on up.

A set of huge snarling teeth met her at the head of
the stairs. She was a split-second away from screaming out loud. Shining black eyes fixed her with a fierce
stare. But no claws came tearing at her. No growl
rang in her ears. The teeth and eyes belonged to a
stuffed tiger, fixed to a plinth, and a second glance
showed her that its skin was lumpy and badly moth-
eaten. She patted the poor creature on the head and
skipped past.

Two long corridors stretched in opposite directions. Clemency was still deciding which to take, when a door opened down the right-hand corridor and the other housemaid, Mary, came out. She carried a full dustpan in front of her and kept her head down. Clemency leapt back out of sight. There was a large table on the landing, bearing a glass display-case filled with stuffed birds. She ducked underneath it. A moment later, the maid's skirts rustled past, her boots light on the carpet, heading towards the stairs.

When she had gone Clemency darted down the right-hand corridor. If Mary had come from the Blue Room, at least she wasn't there any longer. And the aunt must be up here somewhere, if her dogs regularly left hairs on the sofas. She tiptoed down the carpet, listened at the first door she came to and, hearing nothing, gently turned the handle.

The room was decorated entirely in shades of pink: pale pink wallpaper, deep pink carpet, rose satin curtains, raspberry silk sofas. Tall windows overlooked the park, where frost was melting in the bright winter sun. She crossed the room to take a look, hoping to get an idea of the geography of this part of the grounds. As her feet sank noiselessly into the carpet she became aware of voices somewhere nearby. To one side a pair of doors, open a crack, led into the next room. Clemency crept towards them. One voice was rather high, yet crackly, like an ancient little girl. She could just make out the words:

'. . . enjoyed their breakfast?'

'Oh, yes, Miss Lestrange. They ate up every scrap.'

This voice was familiar. Clemency put her eye to the crack between the doors. All she could see was part of a blue velvet sofa, empty except for a tasselled blue cushion. The voice she recognized belonged to Miss Clawe; except that, instead of her usual abrupt manner, Miss Clawe was answering in the most syrupy of tones.

The other woman spoke. 'And have they had their walkies?'

'All except Miss Tigerlily. She wouldn't even put her nose outside the door. Too cold for her, I dare say.'

They must be talking about the dogs, Clemency thought.

'Poor darling Tigerlily! Didn't you like the coldy-woldy? Did that wicked Clawe try and make you go out?'

Miss Clawe's voice wobbled with concern. 'No, Miss Lestrange, I most certainly didn't make her do anything she didn't want to.'

'You'd better not. Now, I think it's time to make them look beautiful. Clawe, hand me the basket.'

Clemency shifted her position. Now she could see the end of the sofa, and a very small person perched on it, her tiny feet barely reaching the floor. She was dressed in an extraordinary outfit of gathered green silk, all bows and frills and fringes that trembled as she moved. And this strange creature, with her quavering voice, must be her aunt, Honoria Lestrange.

She watched as her aunt lifted the lid of a wicker basket, and took out a brush. A pair of hands in black net mittens gently lowered a small furry dog on to her lap. The dog lay across the green silk skirts and submitted to the brushing. It even looked as if it was enjoying the whole business, stretching out luxuriously and turning to look at the human face which gazed back down.

'Oh, Shu-shu,' said its mistress, 'what's this you've got stuck to your lovely coat?'

Miss Clawe apologized. 'I'm afraid Master Shu-shu took himself off into some prickly bushes on his walk this morning, and wouldn't come out. I had to call one of the footmen to extract him.'

Clemency heard a sharp crackling laugh, like ice snapping. 'My naughty Shu-shu. I hope no damage was done?'

'Nothing to speak of, Miss. Just a nip on his hand.'

'I didn't mean the footman, you fool!'

For the next few minutes there was silence, while the dog continued to wriggle and stretch and Honoria brushed his coat and tickled his ears. Another dog slithered around her feet, trying to get her attention. 'You must wait, you impatient boy,' Honoria cooed. Clemency thought that perhaps Miss Clawe had left the room. Might it be the moment to step forward and introduce herself?

But Honoria's voice came again, much harsher this time, asking, 'And what of our little nuisance, Clawe?'

Clemency shivered. Perhaps Honoria was just talking about another dog. She took her eye away from the crack in the door and glanced behind her, feeling suddenly unsafe.

There was a short pause before Miss Clawe answered. 'All is well, Miss Lestrange.'

'I trust it is,' Honoria's frosty voice replied.

'Mrs Curd keeps her busy and out of sight. The reports from Southampton were correct. She is a feeble little thing, small of stature, quite unused to hard work or any discomfort.'

'Discomfort?'

Miss Clawe explained, her voice a little nervous now, 'I only meant that India is hot, Miss Lestrange. Unlike Somerset in winter.'

They were talking about *her*. And Miss Clawe was telling lies, for all was not well, and she knew it—though she didn't yet know quite how badly things had gone wrong.

Her aunt was speaking again. 'So the plan is working. And my brother suspects nothing?'

'No, Miss Lestrange. Mr Theodore is very busy about his own pursuits.'

'How is he this morning?'

'As well as ever, I believe, Miss.'

'How tiresome. Will I never be rid of him? He always was a lazy, sickly thing, and yet he's still here. But I—I am as strong as a horse, and I intend to outlive him by a great many years. Yes, I shall, shan't I, Shu-shu? We'll beat him in the end, won't we, my darling? You may take him now, Clawe.'

Miss Clawe's hands removed the dog gently, and another immediately leapt up on to the green silk lap.

Honoria's voice crackled out fiercely, 'But we cannot have any mistakes, Clawe! Tell me instantly if anything goes awry. If it does, we will have to think again.'

'Please don't trouble yourself, Miss. You know you can leave everything to me.'

Clemency shifted her weight from one foot to the other. The floor creaked. But no one could have heard, for her aunt finished with that subject and turned to another.

'And what news of the old man?'

'Nothing at all to report, Miss Lestrange. Tam Jenkins would have been down to the Little Hall, but he was off on his travels for you.'

Clemency began backing away from the doors on silent feet. She didn't want to hear any more. She didn't need to. They had said enough to make her position clear. But she *did* need to get away, while she still could. There would be no safety for her here above stairs, no more than there was down in the servants' quarters. She had crept most of the way across the room when she heard more voices, this time in the corridor outside.

'No sign of her at all.'

'No, me neither.'

'Oh, lumme! Does the Clawe know yet?'

'No, and I'm not going to be the one to tell her.'

'One of us has to.'

'Not me. You do it.'

'No fear. You can.'

'That rotten little kid! We're both for it now. What are we going to say?'

'That we looked in the laundry and the skivvy had gone—vanished into thin air, like a magic trick. We'll say one of us was outside all the time.'

'She'll know we weren't. She always finds out.'

'Then have another search around. We may yet find her, and Clawe need never know.'

'Just wait till I get my hands on that kid. She'll wish she'd never . . .'

Clemency scrambled under the nearest sofa, squashing herself right up against the wall. From there she could see the pink carpet stretching away, and the double doors to the Blue Room. Perhaps no one would think to come in here at all.

But as she squinted out, she saw a small black nose push its way firmly through the gap between the doors, followed by two glistening black eyes and a pair of silky apricot-coloured ears. The dog cocked his head with interest, then pushed the rest of himself through. He swished across the floor and made his way unerringly to where Clemency was hiding, and began to investigate her boots. She wiggled a foot, trying to push the creature away. He seemed to think this was a delicious game. She pushed again, and felt his tough little jaws fasten round her toe.

Clemency could see how wide the gap was now between the doors; she could even see the blue carpet on the other side. A thin voice cried, 'Ping-Ping? Ping-Ping! Where have you got to, naughty boy?'

Delighted with his find, the dog wriggled further under the sofa and slithered right up to her face. Clemency found herself staring into the snub-nosed, frowning features of a Pekinese. 'Go *away*!' she breathed.

A pair of feet and the hem of a raven-black skirt appeared in the doorway. Miss Clawe's voice, syrupy again, called, 'Master Ping-Ping? Your mistress wants you.'

Clemency grabbed the dog by his collar. He licked the end of her nose. She rolled him on his back, pushed him hard and watched him catapult out from under the sofa, bowling over the pink carpet into the middle of the room.

'Master Ping-ping, *there* you are.' Miss Clawe leaned down and grabbed him firmly with both hands. Clemency could see her black net-covered fingers pinching through the apricot fur. Miss Clawe's voice, low and rough, had no syrup in it now.

'I've got you, you wicked dog. Think you can get away from *me*?'

And she gave the creature a little shake before she carried him back into the Blue Room and elbowed the door shut behind her.

Chapter 18
Uncle

━━◦━━

Safe for the moment, Clemency clambered out from her hiding place. The maids' voices had long since faded away. She opened the door an inch, listened again, then stuck her whole head out. Not a soul. Her first impulse was to run. Then she thought, I am dressed as a housemaid—I should act like a housemaid. That is the best disguise.

She smoothed out her apron, adjusted her cap, and walked back past the glass case of stuffed birds, past the lumpy tiger, to the head of the stairs. Below, a black-and-white shape flitted across the hall: Nancy or Mary, still searching. She daren't go downstairs, not yet, even if that's where the doors were, the doors to outside and escape. So she turned down the left-hand corridor. If the other was her aunt's wing of the house, this must be her uncle's.

Halfway down it, she heard the sound of a door-handle turning. China clinked behind her, between her and the landing, between her and any hiding place. Up ahead there were only doors and more doors and the bare corridor stretching away. All she could do was open the nearest one and slip inside. There were so many rooms that most of them must be empty, she thought. Please let this one be.

Just inside the door was a black lacquer screen. It hid the room from her view completely, and hid her from the room. She held her breath and listened: the air beyond was silent and still. With a sigh of relief she began to breathe normally.

'Yes?' enquired a voice from within the room.

Clemency held her breath again, but couldn't help pulling an anxious face. Perhaps if she kept quite still whoever it was would think they were mistaken.

'Come out where I can see you.'

The voice was sharp and determined. The next moment they might peer round the screen and find her. She had to step out into the room.

A small man lay full-length on a brocade couch. He was dressed in black with an embroidered waistcoat and fancy cuffs. His face was papery-white and he peered at her through a pair of eyeglasses held on a long wand. Somehow Clemency knew at once that this must be Mr Theodore Lestrange. His voice had the same thin, sharp tone as his sister's.

'Yes?' he said again impatiently.

She had a brainwave. 'I'm the new housemaid. *Sir*,' she added, quickly.

He examined her minutely through his eyeglasses for some time, then asked, 'Why don't you bob?'

'Why don't I *what*?' asked Clemency, forgetting her humble housemaidish manner.

'Bob.'

'Bob?'

'Have you come straight from some farm or hovel? Haven't they taught you to drop a little curtsey to your betters?'

Remembering long-ago dancing classes in which she and Phoebe and Tom and Arthur Glover-Smith circled each other, glowering like tigers, Clemency picked up her skirts and dropped the merest hint of a curtsey.

'Very pretty,' said Mr Theodore grimly.

Clemency stood rooted to the spot, wondering how she could get away.

'Did you bring the post?'

'The post?'

'I thought you might have brought the early post,' Theodore said peevishly. He began to fidget with his cuffs. 'It's such a worry. Letters can so easily go astray. Who knows what might happen if they fell into the wrong hands?'

He turned back to the book he had been reading, and exchanged his spectacles for a magnifying glass, which he took from the table beside him. Clemency saw that the room was full of lenses of all descriptions. There was a brass-bound spyglass on the floor near Theodore's feet, and on a table by the window stood a variety of shapes and sizes of prisms. They looked like great chunks of ice. She had no idea what they were for.

Theodore looked up again and said in a bored voice, 'What—are you still here?'

'Yes, sir,' Clemency replied, remembering how she should behave. 'You didn't say I could go.'

'If not the post, what did you bring?'

'I didn't bring anything, sir. I came into the wrong room by mistake. It's my first day here. I'm sorry, sir.'

'Your first day, did you say? A housemaid, eh?'

'Yes, sir.'

'And what is your name?'

If this was her uncle, then he too might be plotting against her. She hadn't had time for everything she'd overheard to sink in, let alone work out what it meant, but she certainly wasn't going to give herself away this time until she knew it was safe.

'Ann, sir,' she said, pulling a name out of the air.

'Ann what? Ann Curd? Ann Clawe? Ann Jenkins?'

'No, sir. Ann . . . Brown.'

'Not related to any of the Curds or the Clawes or the Jenkinses?'

'No, sir.'

'Not got here by any influence of theirs? Or any of the rest of the pack that run this house?'

'No, sir.'

He stared at her. 'You don't sound as if you hail from Somerset. From what part of the country do you come?'

'From much further away than that, sir.'

'And how do you find this delightful house?'

'I can't say, sir, being new, sir.'

Clemency found she was almost enjoying herself. The maids were frantically searching for her, Miss Clawe thought she was scrubbing sheets in the laundry, and here she was talking with the master of the house, calm as you like, and telling him a pack of lies!

'Have you come across my sister yet, Ann Brown?'

'Miss Lestrange? No, sir.' Which was sort of true, since she'd been on the other side of the door.

'Or any of her dogs?'

'I . . . I . . .'

'You'd know it if you had. They *bite*.'

'I've not been bitten yet, sir.' Not really, he only tried my boot.

'Oh, you will. You will. Snappy little beasts, they go for anything they can reach. But no one must ever snap back, you see, for they're my sister's pride and joy. Loves them like she'd never love a brother or a sister—or a child. Foolish woman!' Theodore tapped the side of his nose. 'I'll let you into a secret. All the servants, excepting one or two, are in league with my sister. All these servants work under Housekeeper Clawe. You've met *her*, surely?'

Clemency nodded.

'Miss Clawe is a very unpleasant woman, very unpleasant indeed. Will you like working for a very unpleasant woman, Ann Brown?'

Clemency felt that she ought to shake her head at this point, and did so very heavily and with a solemn expression.

'And yet my valet, quite equal to Miss Clawe in importance, is a very *pleasant* man. Most just and fair, and

not at all a slave-driver.' He paused to let this sink in.
'Now, I know that in theory you will take orders from
Miss Clawe. But it could be most *rewarding* . . . ' here he
leaned across his low table and flipped open the lid of a
silver box which contained a glistening array of candied
fruits, '. . . *most* rewarding to speak to my valet from
time to time, to see if there are any tasks he needs you
to do. And to let him know any little scraps of gossip
from the rest of the household. Especially anything
my sister gets up to . . . Do have one,' he invited her,
indicating the silver box with a languid hand.

Clemency reluctantly took an apricot. After the
peaches last night she was rather sick of preserved
fruit.

'Do you take my meaning, Ann Brown?' Theodore
demanded. He murmured to himself, 'She doesn't look
very bright, but she'll have to do.'

'Yes, sir, I think so. You'd like it if I watched and
listened and reported back to your valet, sir, on the
things Miss Lestrange and the others get up to.'

Theodore looked rather startled. He picked up his
magnifying glass again and stared at Clemency through
it. All *she* could see was his one enlarged eye, and his
white face looming around the edge.

'Astonishing!' he muttered. 'Perhaps you'd better report straight to me, since you've such a good grasp of matters. Never mind the valet. Come straight to me.'

He set his magnifying glass down on the table with some care, then swung his legs off the chaise and seized the long spyglass. Clemency had been wondering from his previous position whether he had the use of his legs at all, but now he walked over to the window and lifted the spyglass to his eye.

'Is there anything else, Ann Brown?' he asked.

There were a hundred things she wanted to know, but at present there was only one thing she could ask.

'Please, what are those things for, sir?' She pointed at the prisms.

Theodore picked up one of the glass icicles and placed it on the window sill. The sun, catching it, sent a rainbow of colours across the ceiling, each one quite distinct.

'Charming, isn't it?' he said, and without thinking she replied, 'Quite delightful.'

As she slipped away behind the screen he raised his spyglass in her direction with a puzzled frown.

The window was at the top of a narrow staircase and

overlooked the distant kitchen garden. From here Clemency could make out Jem, the white-haired gardener's boy, pushing a loaded wheelbarrow, and Mr Ermine pointing to where it should go. It looked a perfectly ordinary day out there. Then, peeping down into the yard below, Clemency spotted one of the outdoor men crossing the cobbles. She quickly drew back out of sight. A door banged downstairs, a drain gurgled. A perfectly ordinary, busy day; except for her.

The stairs, wooden, uncarpeted, led to the servants' quarters, but she couldn't go that way—there were just too many people down there. Instead she turned down a deserted corridor. Here she found a series of unused bedrooms, which faced on to the park. She explored them in turn. The blinds were drawn half down and the furniture was shrouded in white sheets. Dust coated every windowsill and mantelpiece, telling her that it was a long time since any maid had been sent up here with brushes and brooms. The Lestrange family obviously never had visitors to stay. Her uncle and aunt kept to their own parts of the house, solitary and suspicious, caring only that the other should not get the upper hand.

The sounds of the household were very far away; the loudest noise was that of her own stomach grumbling.

Hours had passed since breakfast and she was starving. Thirsty, too. She peered into every jug and basin she came across, but all they had in them was dust, and one had a dead fly at the bottom. Pulling open a bedside drawer, she discovered a stale biscuit, but when she put it between her teeth it was as hard as a fossil. The candied apricot Theodore had given her seemed delicious now. Her stomach growled again just at the thought of it.

Giving up, Clemency flung herself down on a sheet-draped bed. The frame creaked, but no one would hear. She dragged a bearskin rug from the floor and over her legs to keep herself warm. For the time being she was safe, while she pondered on what she'd learned that day and tried to work out what to do next. There wasn't a single person in the house she could trust, except for Poll—and what could Poll, the lowliest of all, do to help her? All her tired and hungry mind could think was: get food, get drink, and then, somehow, get *away*. But where, in all the world, could she go?

At Shaftesbury one of the drum-skins split. At Shaftesbury Alf wrenched his shoulder pulling Whitby up on to the horse to take their curtain call. At Shaftesbury

Jerry tripped over doing his tomahawk dance and the audience laughed at him. Not that there were many in the audience. At Shaftesbury the Red Indians were not very happy.

'A week at Bath,' Jerry reminded the others, trying to cheer them up. 'We'll have rooms at Bath. Proper beds. And stables for the horses.'

'And bills to pay an' all,' said Alf.

Fred was missing Josephine and wondering how the new baby was doing.

'It's all very well in the summer, this lark,' Alf went on, 'but we shouldn't be touring like this in winter.'

'What we need is to cut the horses out,' said Fred.

'What we *need*,' said Alf, 'is a dirty great tent.'

Potter, who had seemed to be asleep, sat up at this point and said, 'The horses are an essential part of the act,' and then fell asleep again.

But Gully was feeling a bit more hopeful. Tomorrow Jerry would help him find the way to Caredew and the Great Hall. Tomorrow, at any rate, they would *know something*.

Chapter 19

Thunder and Lightning

———❘❘○❘❘———

The noise of a heavy bolt being slotted into place cut through the silence. Another, and another, then the rattle of a giant key turning in its lock. A moment later a clock began to strike, resounding eleven times.

Clemency stood in darkness at the top of the great staircase. Below, the old manservant with the stooped back shuffled across the hall and out of sight, clutching his bunch of keys. The house was shut up for the night, thoroughly locked and bolted. Eleven o'clock. She wondered how long before the last servant went to bed. And how long before they slept, dead to the world and to any noise she might make.

On the landing table a single dim lamp glowed. Beside it, matches and tapers. Clemency didn't dare take the lamp, but she grabbed some matches and hurried back the way she had come. In the bedroom where she had hidden was a many-branched candlestick, and she had a plan.

'Wake up!'

Poll woke with a start. Her eyes widened and she shrank back against the wall. Clemency looked down at herself in the flaring candlelight. She had on a white dust-sheet tied like a Roman toga, with the bearskin rug, complete with the bear's head, draped over her shoulders for warmth. Her pale hair stood out in all directions. She realized she must look like a ghost—or an avenging angel.

'Don't be frightened, Poll. It's *me*.'

Poll scrambled over the bedding and stared at her. 'Where did you get to, Flea? Miss Clawe was in a rare old temper. She went on at Mrs Curd, whisper-whisper-whisper, until old Mother Curd put her hands on her hips and told her out loud: "If you want my opinion, that child couldn't stick scullery-maiding and she just run off. She'll catch her death and freeze in a hedgerow, I'll be bound," she said. And she nodded at me, as if to say: Let that be a lesson to you, Poll Flett. So I thought you must be dead, or as good as.'

'I'll be dead of starvation if I don't get something to eat, and quick.' Clemency spied a cup of water beside Poll's chair. Balancing her candlestick, she bent and snatched it up, draining every drop. 'I've been in hiding all day and haven't had a thing. We can raid that larder again.'

'Oh no, Flea. I've had enough of your adventures. I'm not creepin' round anywhere tonight, specially not that old larder.'

'I got you out of trouble this morning, didn't I?'

Poll looked sulky and said nothing. But she reached for her apron and felt in the pocket, pulling out a stale bread roll and handing it over. 'I saved this, I dunno why. I just thought maybe . . .'

Clemency wolfed it down. 'You're a true friend, Poll.'

'Mary the housemaid was whisperin' about you, too. Said you didn't care for the punishment Clawe set you and ran away, most like. That you'd have fell in a ditch in the dark and drowned by now. But Nancy, the one that's so hoity-toity, she said: No, if it was her she'd have hid in a barn or someplace like that. And Mary said, well, the dogs will find her then. Miss Clawe won't stop still she's got back.'

'Dogs?'

'The outdoor men have got dogs. Terriers and such, for sniffin' things out. Rats, and rabbits.'

'So no one thinks I'm still in the house?'

Poll shrugged, and chewed her lip. 'Why *are* you still here if you're in such bad trouble?'

I've got nowhere else to go, Clemency thought bitterly. And, in a way, it *ought* to be my home. It's the only one I've got now.

'Come with me and I'll explain. If you don't dare go near the kitchens, Poll, I'll show you the world beyond them, the world you've never seen. I'll even show you where those spoilt little dogs live.'

Poll stood up. She was terribly afraid of being caught, but even more afraid of missing something thrilling if she didn't go with Clemency. The last couple of days had been the most exciting and unpredictable she'd ever known.

'Here, put this on, or you'll freeze.' Clemency wrapped the bearskin round Poll's thin shoulders.

'I just know we'll be killed,' Poll hissed, but followed Clemency all the same.

The hallway looked even bigger in the flickering candle-light. Its high spaces were caves of darkness reaching out of sight. The shadows of the two girls fell shivering away from them, enormous.

'It's—it's like a *church*,' Poll breathed.

Clemency lifted the lid of the big china jar. 'Look, this is where I hid my old clothes. And spares, just in case.'

Poll peered inside. 'Case of what?'

'In case I needed a disguise. I can hardly run away dressed in a maid's uniform. But I don't know where I can go—and I certainly don't want to die in a ditch.'

Poll gave her stricken look. 'Flea . . .' she said.

They crossed the hall to a giant pair of double doors that opened without a sound. Beyond was a great dining room.

'I've explored upstairs,' Clemency said, 'But I've not been down here yet. Look!'

A dining table the size of a small ship stretched the length of the room, its polished surface shiny as glass. At either end stood a vase of hothouse flowers, and in the centre a dish piled with fruit. Clemency tore off some grapes and shoved half of them into Poll's hand.

Poll pulled back. 'I mustn't!'

'Yes, you must. Nobody will miss them.'

Clemency paced back and forth, eating hungrily, and examining things. On the sideboard there were silver bowls filled with preserved fruit, nuts, and chocolates. The candied fruit reminded her of Theodore. She turned back to Poll. 'I saw Mr Theodore today. I even spoke to him. He thinks I'm a housemaid.'

Poll stuffed a couple more grapes into her mouth. 'But you're only a scullery maid, and a poor one at that.'

'No. I'm not really any kind of maid. That's what I need to explain. You see, my mother grew up here. Honoria Lestrange is my *aunt.*'

Eyes popping, Poll glanced back at the double doors, afraid that at such blasphemy someone would be sure to dash in. But the house remained still and silent.

'When my mother got married she went to live in India, and that's where I was born.' Clemency described the train of events which brought her to Southampton. 'Then Miss Clawe came and fetched me, and I thought my troubles were over. But it was a kind of trick, for as soon as I got here she put me to work in the kitchens, with you.'

Poll's mouth fell wide open with amazement. Clemency dropped a chocolate mint in it.

'I've never heard such a story in all my life,' Poll mumbled. And she had never tasted such a rich taste, either, as chocolate mint.

Clemency bit into a russet-skinned apple. Through mouthfuls she said, 'Well, it's true. I thought Miss Clawe might be hiding me away from my aunt for some secret reason of her own. But I overheard them today, and Honoria knows all about it. She's part of the plot. I don't understand why—not yet.'

She pushed open the next pair of double doors. These led into a magnificent drawing room. The white plaster ceiling looked like an elaborate iced cake. Gilded chairs and sofas and little tables stood around in groups as if they were having conversations. The walls were filled with paintings. Poll stopped in front of a portrait of a very plain couple in old-fashioned dress, both wearing grey powdered wigs.

'Who are these, then, your granny and granfer?' she asked, choking on her giggles. 'They don't look much like you.' She didn't know whether to believe Clemency's story or not.

'I've no idea. But I suppose we must be related somehow.'

They continued around the room. Clemency said, 'I wonder if there's a portrait of my mother here?'

Poll yawned. 'There's gaps, and dark squares on the paint.'

'They've taken some of the pictures down,' Clemency agreed, gazing up at the blank spaces. 'I wonder why?'

'Or did you steal 'em, along with all that other stuff?'

Clemency laughed. She sank down on a plump arm-chair and swung her feet. 'Why d'you think my aunt wants to punish me, Poll? What have I done wrong?'

Poll tested another chair with her fingertips, then sat down, too. She bounced on the cushion and patted the arms.

'You don't have to have done nothin',' she said. 'I'm stuck in the kitchen and I never did anything wrong, did I? It's just how life is.'

'You do believe me though, don't you, Poll? I wish I could prove it somehow.' Clemency looked round restlessly at the walls. 'I wish I could find a portrait that looked just like me, or had my mother's name on it.'

They were both silent for a while. Clemency's stomach, full now with a heavy mix of chocolate and fruit, made a deep grumbling growl. It sounded just like Ping-Ping when he got hold of her boot.

Poll had been thinking. She said, 'Maybe it's because you're you. *If* you're who you say you are.'

'What do you mean?'

'The mistress loves her dogs as if they're people. And she don't care for people at all. Then you come along out of the blue, when she thought you were the other side of the world and never would be a bother to her.'

'I don't think she knew I even existed, until I washed up at Southampton. I don't think either of them knew a thing about my mother's life in India. Just as I didn't know a thing about them.'

'Even worse, then. Suddenly you arrive, come to steal their fortune off 'em.'

'But I didn't know there *was* a fortune!'

'Neither of them's married, no kiddies—except you.' Poll bounced again on her cushiony chair, and said, 'Oh, I *am* goin' up in the world!'

Clemency was thoughtful.

'I saw those dogs today. They're little and fluffy with grumpy faces. One of them tried to bite me.'

Poll laughed. 'Got reason to, now, ent they?'

Clemency stood up, took her candlestick and marched back to the hall. 'Come, I'll show you where they live. They don't exactly eat off tables, but they lie about on silk cushions.'

Poll followed at her elbow. 'I'm not going up them stairs, Flea. Someone's sure to wake up and find us.'

She was still swearing that she would not venture upstairs as she trailed behind Clemency up the double staircase—for Clemency had the only light.

A fusillade of white bullets crashed against the window. They both jumped, and the candles fluttered out.

'Hailstones!' Poll cried in a strangled whisper.

They groped their way towards the top of the stairs.

'There's a lamp up there, and matches on the table,' Clemency said, 'but watch out for the tiger!' She got her hand over Poll's mouth just in time. 'He eats people,' she breathed into Poll's ear, and the two girls collapsed against each other, trying to stifle their laughter. The mix of terror and excitement was making them hysterical.

Clemency lit her candles again, and waved them aloft.

'I found a Pink Room, and along further there's the Blue Room where the dogs were.' She counted doors. 'In here—'

Just as she opened the door, lightning struck and thunder clapped right overhead. Under the vivid illumination of the lightning flash what they saw was not an empty blue drawing room, but an icy-white bedroom and a bed piled high with pillows, on which lay—a *creature*!

The lightning gone, the room fell dark again. Clemency groped behind her for the door handle and the way out. Too late, for the creature was rising up in bed and opening its mouth to scream!

As quick as lightning herself, Clemency darted forward and stuffed the end of her sheet-toga into the creature's mouth. 'Not a sound!' she hissed, and peered at what they had found.

It was her aunt, though barely recognizable as the silk-frocked little woman Clemency had seen through the gap in the drawing room doors. Collapsed like a ragdoll against her mound of pillows, she seemed lost in the huge frills of her nightgown. Her face was the colour of putty, and her eyes started out of her head.

Clemency waved the candlestick above her own head, high enough to keep her features in shadow. They did look an extraordinary sight, Poll with the jaws of the bearskin rug pulled down over her face and its paws tied round her middle, and Clemency wild-haired in her ghostly robe. With sudden inspiration, she howled, 'We are the wraiths of night!'

On no account must she or Poll be caught, especially poor Poll. Her aunt must be terrified into silence—and she was fairly sure they were halfway there already. Still, she waved the candles again to scatter more confusing shadows, and accidently pulled the sheet-gag away. Honoria's mouth stayed wide open but no sound came out.

Clemency hissed, 'We come to warn you, Honoria Lestrange . . .'

Lightning flashed again, then the sea-crash of thunder. All that escaped from Honoria's lips was a tiny yelp.

There was a stirring round Clemency's feet. She looked down to see two Pekinese dogs sniffing her toes. More were snuffling at Poll's bearskin rug. She tried to nudge them away. One of them made a rumbling noise in its throat. If we were really supernatural beings, she thought, dogs wouldn't be sniffing and growling at us, they'd have slunk off into a corner with their fur on end.

Hurriedly she went on, '. . . to warn you of your misdeeds. Foul plans and evil tricks cannot help you. In the end you must come to *this*!'

She held the flickering light over Poll's head. The flames gleamed eerily on the bear's yellow teeth and Poll's terrified eyes glittering behind them.

The dogs abandoned her feet and rushed under a chair. They were fighting over something. She would have to be quick. She leaned towards her aunt and said in a stage whisper, 'You will pay for your evil deeds, Honoria Lestrange. When children suffer, they *remember*. . .' She turned round, shoved Poll in the stomach and breathed, 'Get out, quick!'

They fled, slamming the door shut behind them just as another tremendous thunderclap shook the house. Down the corridor they ran, hearts banging like drums. At the far end they flung themselves round a corner and collapsed against the wall, shaking with silent laughter and clutching each other in fear.

'What made you say all that?' whispered Poll. 'However did you think of them things?'

Clemency shook her head in wonder. 'Lucky we got out before those dogs followed us!'

'I chucked 'em me last chocolate, that's why they left us alone.'

'I nearly died when I saw her.'

'I *did* die!' said Poll.

'Do you think we scared her good and proper? Or will she be calling the servants to search the house?'

'I dunno. All I know is that I must get back to me own bed. What about you, Flea?'

'I can't run away just now. They're right, I'll just freeze in a hedge or the dogs will find me. I'll hide up here tonight, and report to Theodore tomorrow. I must find out more about him, and that's the only way I can think of doing it.'

'Be careful, won't you?' Poll's face twisted up with a mixture of loyalty to her friend and desire to get back to her own room before anything worse happened.

Clemency grabbed Poll's hand to keep her a moment longer. 'You see, he might even take my side once he knows what Honoria's been up to. I'll pretend to be the housemaid again and see what he says when I tell him what's going on.'

'Mr Lysander will do that, Flea. He was down there in the servants' hall, reading the newspaper, calm as can be. Mary and Nancy had their heads together whisperin' like thieves, and he sat there as if it was none of 'is business. But I could see that he was earwiggin' too, same as me.'

'Mr Lysander? Is he Theodore's valet?'

Poll nodded.

'Lysander . . . I've heard that name before. No time to explain, though. Go back quickly now. Here's a candle to light you,' and she unscrewed one of the candles from its holder and handed it, dripping, to Poll. She added, with far more confidence than she felt, 'And please don't worry. If you get into trouble, I promise to rescue you.'

As Poll hurried off in the opposite direction, Clemency thought she heard her make a sort of snorting sound—'Huh!'—but she couldn't be sure.

Chapter 20
Buttered Toast

—||O||—

Mrs Potchard liked Paddington Station. From here trains ran westwards into the open countryside, and if you went far enough, to the sea. It always thrilled her to glimpse a patch of dazzling ocean between the hills. But today she was not travelling as far as the sea. And the weather was not sunny and sparkling, just the dismal gloom of a winter's morning. Fog and smoke and steam combined to make a dim cavern out of the great station. Porters and passengers loomed up out of the murk like ghosts.

Mrs Potchard found her platform and hurried down it, gripping her bag in one hand and her ticket in the other. She chose an empty carriage and a seat by the window, facing forwards. A great hissing and clanking indicated that the train was getting ready to start. She rubbed at the misty glass with her glove and saw the guard waiting with his flag, whistle raised to his mouth.

The carriage door flew open and two more passengers—a man and a boy—threw themselves in. Outside the guard blew his whistle and, with a slow, heavy, grinding of the wheels, the train pulled away.

'Caught it by a whisker,' said the man, sounding pleased with himself. The boy plonked down on the window seat opposite Mrs Potchard and stared at her, rather rudely, she thought. He was buttoned up, knee to neck, in a navy-blue overcoat. His head was round as a ball, and his plump chin wobbled as the train shuddered. The tassel on his cap wobbled too. The man settled himself down next to the boy, and they both seemed to contemplate Mrs Potchard, as if they expected something of her.

'He likes a window seat, my boy,' said the man. 'Likes the view.'

'There's very little to be seen at present,' Mrs Potchard murmured.

'Not so keen on having his back to the engine, though,' the man went on. 'Are you, Bertie?'

Mrs Potchard, who felt the same way, smiled pleasantly and gazed at the fog-blanked windowpane. Surely they didn't expect her to give up her seat for a child? She often found, when travelling, that pleasant smiles and keeping silent defeated annoying companions.

'Are you bound for the West Country?' the man asked next, clearly keen to strike up a conversation.

Mrs Potchard nodded.

'So are we.'

So is the train, she thought, but kept it to herself.

'Would that be on business or pleasure? We're visiting Bertie's uncle, aren't we, Bertie?'

The boy nodded, and sent Mrs Potchard a look which told her he found his father just as annoying as she did.

They rushed into a tunnel, and the noise was such that further talk was impossible. Bertie pulled a book out of his coat pocket and began reading, while his father sat and twiddled his thumbs. Mrs Potchard closed her eyes and pretended to doze. In her mind she turned over the possibilities awaiting her in Somerset, and worried about both Gully and Clemency.

When she next opened her eyes, the fog had cleared. There were fields beyond the window, coated with a thin layer of snow, and two new people in the carriage, an elderly couple eating from a picnic basket. She dimly remembered the slowing of wheels and banging of doors which meant another station. Perhaps she really had been asleep.

The man opposite had already buttonholed the new people. Mrs Potchard let her eyelids droop again. But she couldn't shut out the talk.

'He's such a bright boy, our Bertie. Quite the little professor. His mother and I can't keep up, but we want the best for him. And there is a gentleman, a Very Important Person—' he pronounced these words as if in capital letters, '—who is taking an interest in Bertie. A keen interest in his future. We think Bertie may be very well provided for. Indeed, we may all benefit greatly. I cannot say who this person is, or what it will mean for Bertie, not at present, but I am tremendously hopeful. He's a bright boy, with a very bright future.'

The couple with the picnic murmured politely and the woman offered Bertie and his father some seed cake. 'It's nice that your boy's uncle is taking such an interest in his welfare,' she said.

'Oh, the Very Important Person isn't his uncle. Oh, no, no, no!' Bertie's father was almost neighing in delight at her mistake. 'His uncle is hardly important, hardly important at all. But he has *connections*, you see. And his connections are Very Important indeed.'

Mrs Potchard, tired of all this boastful nonsense, got up and took herself off to the dining car in search of a pot of tea.

The heavenly smell of hot buttered toast wafted down the corridor to Clemency as she made her way to Theodore's room. The grapes and chocolate of the night before had left a sick feeling in her stomach, and made her yearn for the plain solid food she had eaten in Mrs Curd's kitchen. Hot buttered toast would be perfect. If she could get her hands on it.

She knocked and entered. Theodore lay in exactly the same position as on the previous day, reading a tiny book with the help of a very large lens. At his elbow stood a tray on which his breakfast—china tea and buttered toast—lay untouched.

'Yes?' he said, not looking up from his book.

'Good morning, sir.' Clemency remembered to curtsey, but he didn't notice.

'Ah, yes.'

'You asked me to come and see you, sir.'

'Ye-es,' Theodore said, still peering through his lens at the page in front of him. 'Here is an interesting thing.' He began to read aloud: '*Feeding as vultures do, on carrion, plunging their beaks into putrid masses of decayed flesh, were they covered with feathers, like eagles and hawks, about their heads and necks, they would soon become clotted with gore, and become an encumbrance to the bird.*'

At last he looked up. 'Their heads are naked, you see, for the very reason of their eating habits.' He glanced at the breakfast tray and added, 'How extraordinarily convenient.'

Clemency didn't know if he meant his breakfast, or the baldness of vultures.

She tried again. 'You told me, sir, to report direct to you.'

'Ah, yes. Ann Brown.'

Clemency was glad he mentioned her alias, for she had quite forgotten it.

'Let me see . . . You were going to tell me of any news among the servants, any little titbits that perhaps I should know about.'

'Yes, sir.' Clemency bobbed her curtsey again since he was looking, then wondered if she wasn't overdoing things.

'Anything to tell?'

He poured some tea, very weak, with lots of milk.

'Oh, yes, sir. There was an upset last evening. A maid's gone missing from the laundry. Miss Clawe is most put out.'

She watched Theodore's thin lips curl up in a smile around the edge of his cup. He did not like Miss Clawe one bit. Clemency was pleased. She hoped he would reward her news with a slice of toast. The melted butter had run down on to the plate and collected in a golden pool. Her stomach rumbled loudly. She covered it up by speaking. 'They say, sir, she might have run away and drowned in a ditch.'

Theodore glanced towards the park. 'She'd have the devil's own job. The lake is frozen—and if the lake has turned to ice so has every last ditch and stream and puddle. One cannot drown in a solid puddle.'

'They say she might have frozen to death, then, sir.'

'Ann Brown!' he said, putting his cup down with a crash. 'This will not do!'

'N-no, sir,' she stammered, not understanding.

'Go over there, by the window. Stand in the light where I can see you. *Ann Brown*, indeed.'

Clemency's legs felt weak, and not just with hunger.

'Ann Brown . . . a new housemaid. *Not* one of the Clawes or Curds or Jenkinses. *Not* from these parts.' Theodore smiled slyly and tapped his nose. 'After you'd gone, Lysander told me there was no new housemaid. This morning he informed me that Miss Clawe was in a rare old temper because a *kitchen skivvy*—not a laundry maid—had disappeared. Which was odd, to say the least. Because in this house a scullery maid could get cooked for supper by mistake, and no one would turn a hair.'

Theodore rose, and came to stand over her. He looked down his long narrow nose and flared his nostrils.

'Yes, I thought as much. You look just like your wretched mother!'

He spat these last words out, and Clemency knew that she was done for. Nobody was going to take her side.

Theodore peered over her shoulder and out of the window. 'Why, even as I speak, they've got the dogs out after you. Look!'

He spun her round by the shoulders, making her legs wobble even more. She saw two men making their way over the snow-speckled lawns, assorted dogs running eagerly ahead of them. One of the men was tall and thin, his coat flapping. The other was rather short and bandy. Were these the same ones who had watched the house in Wentworth Gardens, and followed her and Gully to the park?

'Miss Clawe has the outdoor men searching for you. My word, you must be valuable to her. I wonder if she has plucked up the courage yet to tell my sister?'

He laughed, a wheezing sound, like squeaky bellows. When Clemency dared to look round, he was sitting down again, and had picked up his book and lens. 'Toast?' he asked.

The buttered toast was cold, but she ate it all, scraping up the congealed butter with the crusts. It tasted glorious. Theodore went on reading his bird book, or pretending to. Every so often he would take a sly peep. Catching her wiping her hands on her apron, he said, 'You must have some other clothes. It is most irritating to have my own niece sitting there dressed like a servant. A *crumpled* servant, at that.'

'Well, I haven't,' Clemency retorted. Theodore's sarcastic manner made her feel quite cross. Now that her disguise was uncovered, there was no need to sound humble and polite any more. 'Miss Clawe could have brought my boxes, but I've not seen them since Southampton.'

'Indeed?'

'And I only had one dress fit for an English winter, and that was made for me by the woman I lodged with. But now it's ruined.'

'My sister has provided you with nothing? Hmm, she doesn't seem to have envisaged a long stay here for you.' Theodore spoke in an even slower drawl than usual. 'You see, my sister and I do not speak. Indeed, I haven't set eyes on her for years. At least, not close to. When I'm bird watching I sometimes have the misfortune to turn my spyglass on Honoria as she walks in the gardens or drives in the park, but otherwise . . . It appears to be a family habit, fighting and feuding and irreparably falling out. Why, your own grandf—' He stopped short. 'But that's another story. The Great Hall and its grounds are, thank heavens, large enough for us to live entirely separate lives.'

Theodore picked up his magnifying glass and peered at Clemency through it. She continued to look cross.

'Don't scowl so, child. That expression certainly reminds me of your mother.'

He put the glass down again.

'As I was saying, my sister and I do not speak. I know nothing of her plots and plans. She has the whole pack of servants conspiring with her. I have only Lysander. But Lysander is very loyal. And rather clever. Much more clever than that ghastly Clawe creature.' He sat forward suddenly and waggled his bony fingers at an ornate Chinese cabinet. 'See there, child. Fetch me that book.'

I don't see why I should wait on him, Clemency thought, but she crossed the carpet and stood in front of the cabinet. Beside the book Theodore wanted there was a small double picture frame. In one half was a painted oval miniature of a girl's face, in the other a portrait of a very stern woman in a lace cap. Both had Theodore's long horse-face.

'Who are the ladies in the pictures?'

Theodore sighed and said, 'My dear mother, of course,' then twitched his hand impatiently for the book.

'Is she my grandmother?'

'Certainly not,' Theodore said, coldly. 'Do you know nothing, child?'

'Not a thing,' Clemency replied.

Theodore tipped his head to one side like a bird. Suddenly his eyes gleamed. 'Not a single thing? You didn't know about—any—of us?'

'No. Mama told me nothing about her family in England, and I don't blame her, now I've seen what you're like.'

Clemency wondered if she wasn't learning more about her mother's character too. Mama had no time for children, and always did just as she wished, regardless of what other people wanted. Perhaps it ran in the family. The more Clemency learned about her relatives, the more she realized what a selfish, cruel lot they were.

'Honoria and I share a mother.' Theodore sighed at the injustice of this fact. 'Your grandfather's first wife. Poor dear Mama died when I was nine, and Honoria ten. *Your* mother was the child of his second wife.' Here he began to giggle. It was a strange sound to come from such a miserable face but it was definitely a giggle. 'And a little bird tells me that Honoria has taken down all her portraits, and those of the insufferable Lucie, too. You won't find a likeness of either of them in the whole house.'

Clemency remembered the blank spaces on the walls, shown up by last night's candlelight.

Theodore turned his attention to the book she handed him and thumbed through it. 'Here we are. Cunning old Lysander. Have you seen this before?' He held out a folded sheet of paper.

Clemency opened it and read. It was Mrs Potchard's letter, the one she had written to the Master at the Great Hall, Caredew, and left in an envelope on Hetty's parlour mantelpiece, to be posted if there was no answer to the newspaper advertisements. Of course, Theodore *was* the Master at the Great Hall.

'Yes,' Clemency said. 'Mrs Potchard is the lady who accompanied me from India. I trust that she's been paid her fee by now.'

Theodore giggled again. 'I shouldn't think so. Honoria's famously tight-fisted.'

Then he leaned forward and rang the bell. His valet, ugly, short and broad, and dressed in very formal black, came in.

'Aha, Lysander—we have the girl, at last. You were right about the maid Ann Brown. Now tell her about your sister's adventure.'

Before he could speak Clemency exclaimed, 'Miss Lysander is your sister! I *knew* I recognized that name.'

'Miss Lysander may be his sister, but you should learn not to interrupt,' Theodore scolded her, then interrupted Lysander himself. 'Lysander drew my attention to an announcement in *The Times*. I was certain that the person it referred to could be nothing to do with me, but Lysander persuaded me that we ought to investigate. He discovered that Honoria had sent two men to Southampton to find out what they could. Which was not much, since she runs such a pack of hopeless in-competents! Meanwhile Lysander dispatched his own sister there, a woman of intelligence and discretion. And she brought back news of a small, unaccompanied girl—together with this!'

His voice was triumphant, and he snatched the letter out of Clemency's hand and waved it at her.

Clemency struggled to piece together the story. 'She . . . she *stole* it? Well, what was so clever about that? It was addressed to you anyway. Left alone, the postman would have brought it.'

'Ah, but it doesn't have my *name* on it. Who else's hands might it have fallen into? I could not take the risk.'

Theodore glanced at Lysander, whose face was as blank as a rock.

'This letter doesn't tell you any more than the notice in *The Times*.' Clemency thought that Theodore, for all his superior manner, was really rather dim.

He snatched the letter out of her hand and slipped it back between the pages of the book. 'I had to satisfy myself as to the nature of the difficulty,' he said, 'and deal with it before my sister stepped in. As she so hastily did. But she failed to catch you.'

'Yes, she did. When she sent Miss Clawe for me.'

'Honoria may well have every creature in this household in league with her, down to the mice in the panelling, but she didn't manage to keep you! I've made her look a fool.'

Clemency was becoming more and more exasperated. 'I escaped without your help. I used my own wits and . . . and . . . inner resources.'

'Ha! But where are you now?' Theodore concluded. 'And who in the world knows where you are, except you and me and Lysander? Tell me that!'

Clemency had to admit that here he had won, for she was trapped, and not even Poll knew for certain where she was.

'But why?' she asked. 'Why do you both want to catch me, and hide me, and imprison me like this?'

'Imprison you? *Imprison* you? Whoever mentioned imprisonment?'

Clemency said nothing, and Theodore seemed to fall into a sulk. Lysander stood as still as a statue in the dimmest corner of the room, merging with the shadows.

Suddenly Theodore sat up. 'All this talk has given me an idea,' he said. 'Lysander, take this—this inconvenience—to the tower.'

Chapter 21
The Tower

Once again Clemency felt a hand grip the back of her neck and push her along. A door was opened and she was thrust inside—not this time into a larder, or a laundry, but towards a steep stone staircase. 'Up there,' said Lysander, the first words she had heard him speak. Tripping over her own toes, Clemency tried to obey him.

When Theodore said, 'To the tower!' she had instantly thought of the Tower of London, into which the kings and queens of England had thrown their enemies, and sometimes been thrown themselves. She knew what it looked like from her Palmer's *History of the World*: four-square and forbidding, with the River Thames lapping at its feet and delivering prisoners by boat to the notorious Traitors' Gate.

Theodore's tower was rather different. As Lysander pushed and prodded her up the narrow spiral staircase, she could smell woodsmoke and leather, as well as the chill reek of the stones. At the first level, Lysander wrenched her to an abrupt halt and threw the door open. She saw a room hung and decorated to look like the inside of a tent. Lysander seemed rather proud of it.

'This is where the master takes a nap when he's busy with his ornithological studies. That's birds to you and me. The bed is reputed to be Emperor Napoleon's own campaign bed, which he slept on when he travelled with his invading army.'

'And his *retreating* army,' Clemency muttered, but Lysander, who perhaps had not had the benefit of Palmer's *History* himself, ignored her. Clemency was surprised that he bothered speaking to her at all.

'Not stopping here. Carry on up,' Lysander said, and gave her a push.

The stone stairs wound upwards, making Clemency dizzy. Arrow-slit windows let in thin shafts of light and gave glimpses of the wintry park. Lysander halted again, opened the next door, and thrust her inside. This room was a study, its circular walls lined with bookshelves. In the middle stood a desk on which there were yet more lenses and telescopes.

Lysander picked up one of the spyglasses. 'This one's supposed to be Nelson's very own,' he said.

Clemency was glad to stand still and recover her balance. 'My uncle seems awfully keen on things that have belonged to famous people from history,' she observed.

'Mr Theodore would smoke Good Queen Bess's baccy pipe if someone told him it was the real thing.'

'Is he easily influenced, then?'

Lysander gave her a sharp look and said no more.

Clemency gazed around her. The books were all about birds and Theodore's desk was scattered with notebooks and sketchpads. Three uncurtained windows looked right over the park, beyond the icy lake to the stark woods. No fire was lit in the grate and it was very cold.

'This is one of the oldest parts of the house, built by Sir Egremont Lestrange over two hundred years ago,' Lysander said, again sounding as if he was giving Clemency a tour of his own mansion. He rattled a bunch of keys out of his coat pocket. 'And I'm locking you in.'

'Wait!' Clemency had no idea what she was going to say next; she just wanted to put off the moment when she would be trapped. 'What's going to happen to me?'

Lysander's eyes were unreadable. She noticed he had a wart on his chin. He clinked the keys, searching for the right one. 'I lock the door. You're in here. Nobody knows. That's it.'

'But *why*?'

'Because my master wishes it. And it's my job to do as he wishes.'

With that he slipped out of the door and she heard his footsteps moving away down cold stone stairs. And finally, at the bottom of the tower, the dread sound of a key turning in a lock.

Poll was busy unloading breakfast trays. The mistress had not touched her food.

'Complaining of a bad night,' Mrs Curd said. 'And now she wants camomile tea sent up to calm her nerves.'

The dogs' bowls were licked clean, however. Nothing had upset their appetites. Poll turned to the master's tray. Not a scrap left here, barely even a drop of milk in the jug.

'Whatever next?' Mrs Curd remarked, peering over. 'Mr Theo eaten up his toast crusts!'

Poll carried the plates to the sink, thinking hard. Flea had said that she was to report to Mr Theodore that morning about what the servants were up to. She'd been ravenous last night, stuffing any little sweetmeat she could find. Perhaps she had gone to his room, and sneaked the toast out afterwards and eaten it. There wasn't even a smear of butter left on his plate.

Mrs Curd came back, muttering. 'Now Mr Lysander's just passed in a message to say the master wants luncheon for three sent up. Got visitors. Visitors at the Great Hall? First time in years! I don't know what's come over them upstairs, I really don't.'

Poll had slipped more bread away from the breakfast table, hiding it in her pocket, for when they met up later. Though perhaps she didn't need to, if Flea was intercepting the meal trays. She yawned, the memory of their midnight adventure brighter before her eyes than the greasy sink-water. Honestly—she, Poll Flett, prancing round that great drawing room and remarking on the pictures as if she was one of the gentry, and bursting into Miss H.'s bedroom and scaring the living daylights out of her! It scared the living daylights out of Poll, too, just thinking

about it. She let one slippery plate drop back into the sink
with a splash, and Mrs Curd was behind her, slapping her
round the ear with a damp dish towel.

'You're on your own again, Poll Flett. That means
twice the work, so don't start slacking.'

At that moment the gardener came through the
kitchen door with his basket and Mrs Curd's attention
was drawn away from the scullery maid.

'I s'pose you're going to moan at me about frost or
some such thing again, Mr Ermine, are you?' she said
sourly.

'Not frost, Mrs Curd. Haven't you stepped outside
yet?'

'Stepped outside? When d'you think I get time for
that?'

'There's snow. Just an inch, but bad enough, what
with the ground friz like iron beneath it—'

Mr Ermine would have gone on, but Mrs Curd
stopped him with an angry exclamation.

'What's this? I can't use this! Look at the state of it!'
she cried, throwing down the offending vegetable and
standing back with her fists on her hips.

''S only a parsnip,' Mr Ermine said mildly. 'I can't help
it if it looks like a mermaid's tail. Still tastes as good.'

By now Poll was craning her neck to see what a parsnip shaped like a mermaid's tail looked like, but the cook's bulky shape blocked her view.

'I'll give you a mermaid's tail! Standards have certainly slipped round here. In the old days vegetables all misshapen like this wouldn't have been brought to the kitchen.'

'In the old days, may I remind you, Mrs Curd,' said Mr Ermine, a model of polite calm, 'the head gardener had a whole staff of reliable men under him. I won't hear a word said against Jem, but in the old days it wouldn't have been just one daft boy and one old man, if you gets my meaning. Then you would have had parsnips as straight as a die, and the only things as'd come up mermaid-shaped would've been mermaids.'

Poll was amazed to see Mrs Curd quieten down and agree with him.

'That's true enough. In the old days under Sir Walter this house was run in the proper way.' Mrs Curd lowered her voice, as if remembering something. 'Though we'd be flayed alive now for saying so if we was overheard.' Then, raising her voice once more, asked, 'A drop of tea, Mr Ermine?'

While Mr Ermine was taking his tea, rather slowly, Poll thought, for a man supposed to be so hard-pressed in his work, Mrs Curd was busy at the range. But when she went out, jangling her keys, to fetch something from the larder, Mr Ermine signalled to Poll.

'Whsst! Hwshsh! Over here!'

Poll obeyed, but anxiously, worried that Mrs Curd would come back and find her neglecting her work.

'Where's that girl, that other one as come out to the glasshouses the day before yesterday?'

'Who, Flea?'

'Was that 'er name?'

'We call her Flea, but she said her name was Clemsy or something.'

'Clemsy? What kind of name is that?'

Poll shrugged, trying to back away to the scullery.

'Where is this Clemsy, then?' Mr Ermine went on, determined.

Poll made a desperate face. 'Gone.'

'Gone?'

'I can't say more. *She's* coming.' And Poll shook her head in the direction of the passageway where Mrs Curd's footsteps could be heard.

'Well, if you sees 'er, say Ermine would like a word,' he hissed, and sank his face in his teacup again just as the cook returned.

'Still here, Mr Ermine?' she said, back to her usual sour manner. 'You do surprise me, a busy man like you.'

And with that, Mr Ermine slapped his cap on his head and went out.

Hanging on the back of the study door Clemency found a tweed coat and hat and a woollen scarf. Although they were much too big, she struggled into them, shivering. She was very glad she'd eaten every mouthful of Theodore's breakfast. How long would she have to wait until someone came for her? If, indeed, anyone did.

First she explored the spiral staircase. The door at the bottom was firmly locked, and only darkness to be seen through the keyhole. She climbed the steps again, counting as she went. Twenty-two steps to the room with the campaign bed, twenty-five more to Theodore's study. She looked up, into the twisting darkness above. Her legs felt like jelly, but she continued on up. There might just be a way out at the top. Instead she found a small door set in a stone arch, shut and immoveable. Of course it was, she told herself. Theodore might be dim, but he wasn't completely stupid, and Lysander, as she had been assured, was cunning itself.

Clemency made her way back down to the study. To pass the time, she examined Theodore's books, his sketches, and his bird-watching journals. The books were dull, with tiny print that was hard on the eyes. The drawings were not good. The journals, with entries such as:

5th May. Raining. Heron, later 2 Great Crested Grebe.

6.25 p.m. Heron back again . . .

were hardly riveting. There were one or two letters written in a tidy hand, signed 'Your friend in science, B. Watkyn', but they too were very dry, just about birds or weather or even mathematics, so she tossed them aside. She tried out all the spyglasses, tapped the barometers, and shook the compasses. She spun round on Theodore's revolving wooden chair until she felt sick, and then spun back the other way, which didn't help.

Finally, she got up and went over to the windows. The panes were diamond-shaped, and the glass old and flawed, so that when she looked through it, the park stretched and bent in front of her eyes. The men with dogs were no longer in sight. Nothing moved, except for a few black dots of birds in the distance. She didn't know the names of English birds. Except a pochard, of course, as Gully had instructed her, but there were no ducks at all on the frozen lake.

But something *was* moving: far off, another black shape, too big and square to be a bird. It advanced from the trees, following the line of the carriage road. She made out a big brown horse and a high cab. Minutes passed before the carriage reached the front of the house and pulled to a halt. She thought of her own arrival, and being driven straight into the yard, with no welcome at all.

Another black shape appeared on the gravel, coming from the house. It was Lysander, looking even shorter and broader from this angle. He opened the door of the carriage and helped a small figure down. Clemency pressed her face to the distorted glass to get a better look. It was a boy in a tight navy-blue coat, a podgy boy, wearing a tasselled cap. He was followed by a plump man who shook hands with Lysander. The boy was patted on the shoulder by both men. Then they dis-appeared into the great front door of the house.

Clemency turned from the window, and sighed. 'Well, well. *Some* people come in at the front door. *Some* people are given a proper welcome.' She had no idea what to make of it. Instead, she picked up one of the spyglasses—the one supposed to have belonged to Admiral Nelson—and began to make a thorough sur-vey of the park.

It seemed hours later when she heard a key twisting in the lock and then Lysander's heavy tread on the stairs. When he entered, his expression, far from blank, was very smug.

'Leftovers from luncheon. Game pie and cabbage. There would have been scalloped potatoes too, but they ate the lot. However, the master was so kind as to leave you all his cabbage. And a corner of the pie. There's a bit of stewed apple to follow.'

At least he's not leaving me to starve, Clemency thought.

Lysander cleared a space and put the food down on Theodore's desk. The first course was on a side plate, and the stewed apple in a saucer. Clemency grabbed the pie, all manners forgotten.

'I'm to wait till you're finished.' Lysander said.

Clemency scraped up the last of the cabbage and started on the apple. Lysander had moved away and was running his hand along the oak bookshelves.

'The master's got some very valuable books here.'

'Some very *dull* books,' Clemency said, her mouth full. 'I've had a look at them.'

'You shouldn't be poking about in other people's property. Valuable property that doesn't belong to you.'

Clemency thought about her conversation last night with Poll. 'It may do, one day,' she said.

'I wouldn't be so sure about that.'

Lysander prowled the room, touching a spyglass here, a clock-face there, and puffing out his cheeks to stop himself from smiling. He reminded Clemency of Phoebe Glover-Smith when she had some secret she was terribly proud of, and terribly keen to share. Clemency tried another tack. She stopped scooping up the apple as fast as she could and let the spoon idle in the saucer. He couldn't go until she'd finished. And she might be able to get some information out of him before then.

'I saw a carriage draw up,' she said. 'A very cold day to come visiting . . .'

Lysander's smile vanished. 'Spying, were you?' he snarled.

'Hardly spying. You shut me in this place, with nothing to do but look out of the window.' And read dull books, she added to herself.

'Your mother was a spoiled, wilful little girl, and so arc you!' Lysander said. 'No wonder they hated her so.'

'Did you know my mother, then?' Clemency asked. She tried to arrange her features to look sweet and innocent, but slightly dim. She wasn't sure she succeeded.

Lysander frowned but couldn't help puffing himself up again. 'My mother was a Jenkins. She worked for the family for years, and told me all about them long before I came into service here. What I don't know about them isn't worth knowing.'

'Oh, tell me about my mother. Do, *please*.'

Lysander lounged against a bookcase and began, just as if he was reciting a bedtime story, 'I'll tell you what my mother told me. Sir Walter Lestrange—that's your grandfather—inherited a big house and lots of land, but scarcely any money to keep it all going. So it was only common sense for him to marry a lady with a fortune to her name, which he did. His wife gave him two children, a girl and then a boy. When she died, he married again, very quickly. A charming girl this time, though still with money to her name . . .'

'Was the first one *not* charming, then?'

'No, she was a cold creature, so my mother said. But the second wife . . .'

'My grandmother?'

'Do you want to hear this story or not?'

Clemency clamped her lips shut and waved at him to go on.

'The second wife gave birth to a daughter, then three years later she died too. Sir Walter spent all his affections on this child—a pretty little thing, she was. He let her have her own way over everything, until his other two felt pushed aside. They saw she had a better time of it than they had when they were children, and they were jealous. They forget it was their own mother who made sure they had a rotten time. She was very strict with them. Maybe their father would have spoilt *them* too, if she'd only let him. And maybe little Lucie's mother would have been strict with *her*, if she had lived. Though I don't think she was the sort, from what I knew of her.'

'Little Lucie,' Clemency said, half to herself. 'What happened next?'

'Neither Mr Theo nor Miss H. married, nor do I think ever wanted to. And they certainly didn't want *her* to, when she was old enough.'

'Why not? It would have got rid of her,' Clemency said simply.

Lysander laughed, a snickery, out-of-practice sounding laugh. 'You *are* a chip off the old block, aren't you? Well, they wanted her out of the way, but not if it was something that was going to make her happy. They were all in the business of making each other as unhappy as possible. Still are,' he muttered. 'When she was away on a visit she met someone. Not quite as good as Sir Walter would have wanted for her, but then probably only the Duke of Somesuch or the Prince of Somewhere Foreign would have been good enough in his eyes. But he would have said yes if she stamped her foot hard enough, I'm sure, except that Miss H. and Mr T. were stamping their feet even harder at this end. And Sir Walter was in a real quandary. Never been the type to make up his mind when it mattered. Before anyone knew it, Miss Lucie had run off and married this chap without her father's permission and they were sailing to India out of every-one's grasp.'

'So they're being horrid to me just because they used to be horrid to Mama?'

'Oh, no, not just for that reason.'

'And my grandfather . . . ?'

Lysander straightened up and cleared his throat, as if he had just remembered something. 'Enough. That's all I'm saying.'

He picked up the tray. His voice was gloating. 'It will do you no good, all this spying and prying. No good at all. Too late for that. Your goose is cooked, my girl.'

With that he was gone.

Clemency licked her fingertips in case she had missed any crumbs. I should have asked him to light the fire, she thought. I should have asked him who that boy was. He seemed inordinately pleased with himself, but I've no idea why.

Chapter 22
Making Ripples

—||—o—||—

Dear Colonel Hibbert, Clemency wrote on a sheet from one of Theodore's notebooks. She knew that the letter would take weeks and weeks to get to India, even if she could somehow smuggle it out, and then it would take weeks and weeks for any kind of help to arrive. But she couldn't think of anyone else who cared; and she wanted someone at least to know what had become of her.

> Dear Colonel Hibbert,
> It is my most earnest hope that you remember me . . .

Just thinking about the people she knew in India turned her back into the polite little girl she had been then.

. . . My father was killed the day his horse broke its neck in that awful race you were so cross about. My mother was taking me home to England but unfortunately she died on the way. You may have heard about it from her friends the Cleavers, unless they died too. I am writing to request help in any way you see possible, for though I have found—or been found by—my relations here in England, I am now imprisoned by them and fear for my life.

She bit her lip and read through what she had written so far. It sounded very melodramatic. She only hoped that he would believe her.

I am at the Great Hall, Caredew, near Frome, in Somerset. Should you be able to intervene on my behalf, I beg you not to trust my uncle Theodore Lestrange or my aunt Honoria Lestrange, who are half-brother and half-sister to my mama. They are wicked and cruel and not to be believed. I often think of you, and especially your dear, handsome horse, Treasure. Do give my regards to the Glover-Smiths.

Yours in anticipation,
Clemency Wrigglesworth

She wasn't happy with the letter—it didn't at all convey how desperate she was. Her schoolroom exercises in letter writing had not covered situations like this. But she folded it up and addressed the outside to Colonel Hibbert at her father's regiment, c/o India, sealed it, and put it in her pocket. She would have to wait for a chance to get it out of the house, and at the moment she felt very gloomy about ever achieving that.

That same afternoon Mrs Potchard was sitting in the office of Jeremiah Doggett, Solicitor, in Frome. The one gas lamp barely lit the room, and a small fire flickered dismally. Mr Doggett wore a creased black coat and looked as if he had been sitting in the same position for years on end. He reminded her of an old tortoise.

'I would like your advice,' Mrs Potchard was saying, 'on several matters. First I have some—er, business—with a family in the neighbourhood. Lestrange?'

'The Lestrange family, yes, yes.' Mr Doggett nodded slowly.

'You know of them?' Mrs Potchard tried to sound offhand.

'I have in the course of my career drawn up legal documents for the Lestrange family.' He examined his fingertips. She felt that he could have said more, but was by nature, and profession, very cautious.

'Perhaps I should ask about another matter first,' she went on. 'My son, who is fifteen, and my niece, just two years older, have run away and joined a travelling show. My concern is more with the girl than with my boy. Her mother and I fear she may enter into a hasty marriage with a young man who performs in the show.'

'Travelling show?' Mr Doggett interrupted, leaning forward. 'What kind? A theatre company? A circus?'

'Red Indians,' said Mrs Potchard.

'Red *Indians*!'

'Genuine Red Indians. Or so they say.'

'Don't talk to me about Red Indians,' muttered Mr Doggett. 'I have a son who just a year ago was a good, hard-working, reliable boy. Why, he sat in my outer office, just there, and kept his head down at his desk. But then he suddenly ran off—with *Red Indians*. Now he can throw a tomahawk like nobody's business. My own boy Jerry!'

'Jerry?'

'Not that he calls himself that these days. Little Owl—or Kitty Hawk—or some such name.'

'Little Hawk.'

'Little Hawk. You may be right.' He fished around in the papers on his desk and eventually uncovered a postcard. It bore a picture of the pier at Brighton.

'I *am* right, Mr Doggett,' said Mrs Potchard. 'For your son's Red Indians and my son's Red Indians are one and the same. And it's *your* son that my niece has her bright eye on.'

'Merciful heavens!' cried the solicitor, knocking over his inkpot and drowning the pier.

Mrs Potchard mopped up the ink while Mr Doggett called out to his clerk in the next room, 'Tea, in here, at once! Strong tea!'

When the tea, which was as brown as a peat-bog, was brought, Mr Doggett raked up the fire and invited Mrs Potchard to sit nearer its warmth. As simply as possible, she explained the story of Clemency from the moment she first set eyes on the child.

'So you see,' she said, 'my dear boy Gully feels responsible for her. He joined the Red Indians as a way to get to Somerset as quickly and as cheaply as he could. But Whitby wanted to join them long before.

Looking for Clemency was just an excuse. Her mother and I disapprove most strongly of her cavorting about the countryside quite unchaperoned.'

'Hmm,' agreed Mr Doggett. 'And I, of course, could not countenance her marriage to my son. Both of them are under age, and, besides, quite mad.'

'They'd make a good pair, then,' Mrs Potchard said into her teacup.

'It's odd that you should mention the Lestrange family,' Mr Doggett murmured. 'I had not heard from them in years, but just an hour ago I received a letter summoning me to see Mr Theodore Lestrange tomorrow morning. Bear in mind, that's not something I would tell just any passer-by . . .'

'But now we find we have far more in common than just passers-by,' Mrs Potchard reminded him. His ponderous manner was beginning to depress her. She could imagine how someone with an adventurous spirit might long to jump up from his desk, abandon those dusty stacks of documents, and run away.

'Quite. They are a somewhat eccentric family. As a legal man I've found them difficult to work for. Miss Lestrange is obsessed with her pet dogs. Mr Theodore turns with any wind that blows. They both have peculiar ideas about what should happen to the Lestrange property, and the fortune, if any of it remains. Each is determined that the other won't get their hands on it. And now here's Theodore—that would be your girl's uncle—wanting to make alterations to his will.'

Mrs Potchard brightened. 'That could be good news, don't you think? With the arrival of Clemency, perhaps—'

Mr Doggett shook his head sadly. 'I feel the arrival of the child would have caused . . . a ripple.'

'A ripple?'

'Perhaps a *stir* would be more accurate.'

'A stir?'

'A smidgen of disturbance,' Mr Doggett decided, pressing the tips of his fingers together. 'And they don't like disturbance of any kind, at the Great Hall.'

'You mean that Clemency's arrival would have been like a bomb exploding in their midst?' said Mrs Potchard, tired of tiptoeing about.

'Er . . . quite.'

'In that case, I think it is in both our interests to get to the Great Hall as soon as possible.'

Mr Doggett looked alarmed. 'No, no, haste would be most unwise. Most unwise. I shall be there tomorrow

morning at eleven. That is quite soon enough.' He un-
folded a letter that sat on his desk. 'Mr Theodore . . . not
that he has written himself, of course. His servant
Lysander sent the letter.'

'Did you say Lysander? Lysander is the name of his
servant?'

'His valet, I believe, and right-hand man.'

Mr Doggett glanced at the letter, but Mrs Potchard
snatched it out of his hand and read the spiky black
handwriting.

'I don't like the sound of this at all,' she said. 'I want
to find my boy Gully. I want to find my niece. But most
urgently of all, I must find Clemency Wrigglesworth. I
think the poor child may be in grave danger.'

She stood up, pulling her gloves on briskly and setting her hat at a sharper angle. Mr Doggett flinched
when he saw her aim the hatpin.

'If you won't come with me, I'll go alone,' she said.

'I most certainly wouldn't advise that. Why, it's
getting dark.'

'Then we'd better hurry.'

Mr Doggett harrumphed several times, puffing
out his cheeks. He clearly could not decide what to
do. Mrs Potchard, used to bending generations of

children to her will, fixed him with her stern eye and said, 'Come, Mr Doggett!,' and he did.

When Poll went to set the table in the servants' hall, she found two strangers sitting there, a man and a boy, the fattest little boy she'd ever seen. She nearly dropped her stack of plates.

'Come in,' the man instructed her. 'Don't let us interrupt your work. We're here to visit Mr Lysander.'

'We're here to visit Mr *Lestrange*,' corrected the boy. 'We had lunch.'

Poll put down her plates, and smoothed out the tablecloth, sneaking sideways glances at the pair. Looks like you've had lots of lunches in your time, she thought. And very good ones, too.

'We've come from London. Have you ever been to London?' the boy asked her. The man just sat back, folded his hands over his silvery waistcoat, and smiled.

'I've never bin anywhere,' said Poll, keeping her head down and crashing a handful of forks together.

The boy laughed, and Poll didn't like the sound of it. Fumbling, she dropped a knife, quickly picked it up, and put it back on the table.

'I saw that!' said the boy. 'That knife's dirty. That won't do.'

Poll snatched it up again, and replaced it with clean one, stuffing the dirty knife in her apron pocket. Know where I'd like to stick it, she thought, screwing up her face with rage but keeping it turned away from the visitors.

'She won't get away with that sort of thing when *I'm* in charge,' the boy said, and the man replied, 'All right, Bertie. All in good time.'

'Well, she won't.'

Poll rushed through the rest of her tasks so that she could get out. The man with the silvery waistcoat stood up and strolled to the door, looking this way and that as if in search of something, or someone. He took out his pocket watch and tapped it. 'We have a train to catch,' he said importantly.

'You going to be the next butler, then?' Poll muttered to the boy as she whisked past him with her empty tray.

'The next butler?' he hissed back. 'No. The next *master*.'

Poll nearly collided with the broad black bulk of Mr Lysander, who was just arriving. She ducked under his arm and rushed off down the passageway, not knowing whether to believe her own ears.

At mid-afternoon, Theodore, closely followed by Lysander and a tea tray, made their entrance. Clemency was glad that her letter was safely out of sight, and the desk arranged just as before.

'My hour for bird watching,' Theodore announced. He was wrapped in a thick overcoat. 'But first, tea. And a little heat, Lysander. It's cold as the grave up here.'

The valet, his face blank as a sheet, stooped to light the kindling, made sure it was burning, and then silently withdrew.

Theodore poured himself a cup and wandered around with it, peering into the books on his shelves. Clemency had an idea. Poll cleared all the trays down in the kitchen—anything on the tray Poll would be bound to find. She would hide the letter somehow and Poll would discover it and post it for her. While Theodore was busy, she tore off a scrap of blotting-paper and wrote on it: *URGENT! Please post this for me. Life or death!! Your friend CW.* She did not put Poll's name on the note just in case it was intercepted by Mrs Curd or one of the other servants. She did not want to get Poll into more trouble.

Theodore came back to the table to choose a biscuit.

'Help yourself to tea, child,' he said briskly. 'You can't always be waited upon.'

This morning I was waiting on *you*, Clemency thought, but she ate a biscuit and wondered where she could hide the letter. It would get wet through if she put it in the teapot or the slop bowl and it might be seen if she slid it beneath a saucer. But the sugar bowl had a lid. Quick as a flash, she emptied all the sugar lumps into her apron pocket, stuffed the letter and blotting-paper note into the bowl, and put the lid back on. When Theodore next turned round, she was busily sucking at a sugar lump, an expression of complete innocence on her face.

'I'm going up on the tower before the light fades,' Theodore said. 'You may come too. I see you're dressed for it.'

He fished out a key from a little drawer in the desk. I wish I'd known that was there, Clemency thought.

They went up the tower stairs until there were no more to climb. Theodore unlocked the small wooden door and suddenly they were outside, on top of a cold grey world that stretched, empty, for miles.

Is he going to push me off? Clemency wondered. She hung back in the doorway but Theodore did not seem concerned with her at all. He raised a pair of binoculars to his eyes and scanned the park. She couldn't work her uncle out; his mood changed in an instant, and she never knew what it would be next.

'Not a bad time for spotting visitors,' he said. 'They get blown here, you see, on the winter winds. Sometimes they come south to feed if it gets too cold in northerly parts. Are you fond of birds?'

'Not particularly,' said Clemency, her teeth chattering with the cold. She recalled her arrival in Wentworth Gardens, shivering and miserable—she had felt so hopeless then. But that was nothing compared to this.

Theodore ignored her lack of interest. He handed her the glasses and said, 'Have a look towards the lake. Never know, might be lucky.'

'What should I look for?'

'Oh, anything unusual . . .'

Clemency raked the horizon with the binoculars. Down near the lake several cold-looking ducks stood hunched on the grass. But something *was* unusual . . . She swung the glasses back and tried to pick it up again. A tall stiff feather sticking up—no, two—behind a bank of grass. She found it again, and focused. No bird, just feathers.

'I think I've found something—ah, no, it's gone.'

The feathers dipped out of sight, then appeared again. Astonished, she made out a dark head beneath them, a *human* head, and then a second, ginger, crowned with a brown cap. Something so familiar about it! Her heart began to thump with excitement. Could it really be? She watched the two heads move cautiously along behind the bank.

'Quick, quick! Hand me the glasses,' Theodore said. 'What is it? What can you see, child?'

But Clemency had no intention of letting Theodore see. She handed over the glasses but pointed his gaze in the wrong direction. 'I thought I spotted some visitors,' she said. 'But it was just a Potchard.'

'There are often mallard on the lake,' Theodore said, anxiously squinting in the failing light, 'but no pochard. You're quite wrong there, you know.'

He shivered too, and pulled his collar up around his ears. 'Absolutely nothing. And it's getting too dark now, and much too cold. I'm going in.'

Clemency followed him down. Her body felt like a stick of ice, but right inside a bright hopeful spark was beginning to catch light.

Chapter 23

In the Bothy

————————————

Poll had never been in the bothy before. She stood in the golden firelight and watched Mrs Ermine kneading dough with supple hands. She had never set eyes on Mrs Ermine either, or even heard of her existence. Mr Ermine sat in front of the fire and his wife, a tiny round figure, stood behind a small table making bread. Everything had to be small in the bothy, including its occupants, because the bothy itself was so small. But it glowed with warmth and was filled with the fragrant smells of the apple-wood fire and the bread-making. Poll wished she could stay there all evening, and never have to go back to her cold bare room.

Mr Ermine contemplated the two pieces of paper that Poll had brought him. It was hard to make them out in the firelight, but he had a better chance than Poll.

'Didn't you ever go to school, then?' he asked her.

'I did, but I didn't never stay for very long.'

'Surely you learnt your letters while you was there?'

'I learnt my letters all right,' Poll said, 'but I never got as far as joining them up into words. I had to stop at home and look after my brothers.'

Mrs Ermine smiled at her encouragingly. 'Where d'you say you found these?'

'In the sugar bowl, the sugar bowl that come down from Mr Theodore's rooms.'

'*Your friend CW,*' Mr Ermine read slowly. 'Have you got a friend called CW?'

'I ent got no friends,' said Poll, shrugging.

'Except young Clemsy,' Mrs Ermine remarked. Her husband had obviously told her all he knew.

'Flea,' said Poll. 'That's another thing. Before I found those papers, I was thinking of coming to see you anyway. I couldn't tell you it all, not in the kitchen this morning. I'd've been killed if Mrs Curd saw me. And there's more than that, even—what I heard just now.'

She stopped, and it was Mrs Ermine who said gently, 'Well, go on, then.'

'Flea's not gone, not really *gone*, see. She's in hiding, in the house. And she was going to see Mr Theodore this morning. And all his breakfast was ate, and his luncheon too—though a nasty boy might've had that—and now these papers appear. And we went all round the house at night, and she looked at the pictures and says they was her family, and we ate the fruit, which didn't count as stealing cos she says it was hers anyway.'

Poll's eyes looked wild with fright and confusion, and Mrs Ermine stretched out a hand and murmured, 'Dear, dear,' in a comforting way.

Mr Ermine only sighed, and muttered, 'I thought as much.' And he reached for a tin on the mantelpiece from which he took a piece of crumpled newspaper.

'See this? I was wrappin' the old geraniums up for the winter and I came across this bit of *The Times*. Miss C. Wrigglesworth and the Great Hall, Caredew, near Frome. That's what jumped out at me, the Great Hall, printed in the paper, y'see? Don't get that every day. So I was wonderin' when this Miss C. Wrigglesworth might turn up and start demandin' peaches and pineapples and I don't know what . . . And then this little girl comes into the glasshouses and began talking to me about tea plants.'

He looked at Poll and tapped the side of his nose. 'Tea plants as grow in *India*.'

Poll was totally at sea by now.

'So I say we ought to open this letter from your friend CW, even though I don't hold with openin' other people's post, in the general way of things.'

While he read the letter, Mrs Ermine said to Poll, 'What struck Mr Ermine was that a kitchen maid should know what a tea plant looked like. So he looked a bit harder at her and what struck him then was that she was the image of Miss Lucie when she was a littl'un. And he thought about that announcement in the paper about Miss Lucie's daughter arriving from India. And he couldn't make it out at all. So he thought he'd have another word with the little girl.'

Mr Ermine interrupted her with a loud grunt.

'Here we have it!' he cried, striking the letter with his free hand. 'Miss Lucie's daughter it is. And Mr Theo and Miss H. knows all about it. Come on, girl, we've an errand to do!'

'I got to get back,' Poll said. 'I should never've stayed this long.'

'No you don't, you're coming with me.' Mr Ermine began to pull on his jacket. 'Off to Molly's,' he said to his wife.

'It's cold out.' Mrs Ermine wrapped Poll up in a shawl and put a spare cap of Mr Ermine's on her head.

'But I can't,' Poll protested, as Mrs Ermine spun her round, tucked the shawl in, and pushed her out of the bothy door. 'Mrs Curd'll kill me when she finds out.'

'Say it's my fault,' Mr Ermine told her. 'Blame me. They always do. Besides, by the time we've finished, they'll all have more to think about than where a skivvy's got to.'

He carried a lantern and lit their way with its swinging light through the kitchen garden. Poll stumbled after him.

'Where are we going?' she whispered.

'We're going to see Molly, down at the Little Hall.'

'The Little Hall? What's that?'

'Never heard of it? If you was a Curd or a Clawe or a Jenkins you'd have heard of it.'

'Well, I'm not!' Poll said, cross that he was getting her deeper into trouble for something she didn't begin to understand.

'An' I thought you stood there in Mrs Curd's shadow with your big ears flappin',' he teased her. 'Poor old Poll, stuck in the kitchen, ent got a clue what goes on.'

He led the way down a path through empty fields. In the lantern light the snow shone eerily.

'I knew about Flea and none of the rest of 'em did,' Poll retorted. 'My heavens, what's that!?'

Two dark shapes loomed up out of the night before her, snorting out white clouds. Mr Ermine stopped and held up the lantern.

'Just 'orses. Though what they're doing here, great parti-coloured beasts like that, I don't know. They're not carriage 'orses, that's for certain.'

Poll ducked past the two huge shapes, and the feel of Betty and Brownie's hot breath on her neck made her shiver with alarm.

'Through here,' Mr Ermine said, holding open a narrow gate for her. The path now ran down the side of a wood. 'There's the Great Hall, see, and the Little Hall, where the family used to live in days gone by, afore they built that great monstrosity. When old Sir Walter fell out with Miss H. and Mr Theo, he packed up and went to live at the Little Hall, with just Molly to take care of him. And he's still there, just about. I bring fruit and vegetables over every day, and Tam Jenkins takes care of the repairs and the heavy work. Apart from that, there's no to-ing and fro-ing between them and the big house at all.'

'And I never heard of it,' Poll said in wonder.

'It all happened a good many years ago. Mr Theo and Miss H. always did dislike each other, and never exchanged a word if they could help it, and their father went the same way when Miss Lucie ran off. A funny old family, they are. But Sir Walter's not so bad.'

They had come to some light. Poll could make out a long low building set in a hollow and hemmed about by dark trees. One or two windows were lit, and Mr Ermine went and rapped on one with his knuckles.

'Molly, it's Ermine. Let us in.'

A round face came to the glass and peered at them.

'Good grief, Mr Ermine, what's going on?'

'You wouldn't believe the half of it, Molly. Let us in before we're frostbit, there's a good woman.'

Lysander had taken away the tea things. Clemency crouched in front of the fire, thawing her fingers. Out of the corner of her eye she saw Theodore put his key back in the desk drawer. He made as if to leave, then paused.

'I had a very interesting interview today,' he said. 'One seldom finds a mind as sharp as one's own. An intellect as questing. It is a sheer delight to converse about the sciences with someone who can . . . Are you listening, child?'

'Oh—oh, yes.'

'So, I have decided. I wouldn't care for all my work here to go to waste.' He waved a hand round at his books and at the papers on his desk, like a king waving to his loyal subjects.

All your hopeless drawings and boring diaries, Clemency thought. She just wanted him to shut up and go, so that she could get on with planning what to do next. Gully was out there, Gully's red head was darting about the park, and he must be looking for her. But while Theodore's voice kept droning on she couldn't think straight.

'I shouldn't want all this to go to dust. I must have someone sufficient to the task to pass it on to. Someone I can train to continue my great work. A scientific mind. An enquiring mind. A truly noble mind.' Suddenly he reached forward and tapped her sharply on the head. 'Not a wicked noddle full of tricks and lies!'

Shocked, Clemency teetered on her heels and sat back with a painful bump.

'My hateful little sister's child will not inherit any of this. You were a nasty surprise, I can tell you, popping up like that from nowhere.' He gave her a suspicious look as if something new had just struck him. 'It wouldn't be beyond belief to assume that you were some sort of trick yourself, and nothing to do with Lucie at all. Just some con man's idea to wrench my fortune from me.'

'But—but—you said yourself that I looked just like her. And acted like her, too.'

'Act? Anyone can act!'

Theodore strode about, waving at his books again. Clemency wondered if he'd actually gone mad.

'I'm talking about true nobility of mind. Lysander, my faithful Lysander, has shown me that there are people in this world fit to follow such a lead as mine. I intend to make his nephew, Bertram Watkyn, my heir. It's unconventional, I know, but not unheard of for an adopted heir to take on the great mantle. An exceptionally bright, well-thought-of boy.' Theodore seemed to run out of steam at this point, as if he wasn't sure that these words were his own.

Clemency pushed herself to an unsteady standing position. 'The boy in the blue coat?'

'The colour of his coat is immaterial.'

'What about me?'

Theodore looked puzzled. 'Oh, I wash my hands of *you*.'

'Does that mean I can go?'

'Go? Go where? Most certainly not. Lysander has a little plan for you. I always leave the tiresome details to Lysander.'

And with that Theodore hurried away down the stairs, clanging the door shut after him, and rattling the key angrily in the lock.

Clemency could not afford to wait for Lysander to carry out his 'little plan'. She shuddered to think what that might be—the orphanage that Poll had described, or *worse*?

She sprang over to the desk. The drawer that held the key was shut tight. It fitted in so neatly with the desk's decorative panelling that had she not seen Theodore open it, she would not have suspected it existed. It had no lock, but there was no handle either, and she couldn't prise it open. She grabbed a ruler and worked at the front panel, but nothing gave way. The drawer must open by some secret device. She threw down the ruler and felt around lightly with her fingertips, running them over the drawer front, the desk panels, the other drawers which opened easily and contained nothing but more notebooks and pencils, ink bottles and nibs. Furious, she sat back and glared at the drawer. She found herself staring at one particular knot in the grain of the wood, a perfect round dark eye, and almost before she realized it her hand had gone to the knot. Her finger pressed the eye, and the drawer slid smoothly open with no effort at all. In it sat the key to the door at the top of the tower.

Chapter 24
Burglars, Devils, Ghosts

—++o++—

Jerry Doggett, alias Little Hawk, in full Red Indian costume, sneaked across the frozen grass, keeping his head low. Behind him, Gully said, 'Your feathers are sticking up. Someone's bound to spot us. I don't know why you had to dress up in all that rig.'

'Because I don't want anyone round here to take me for a solicitor's clerk,' he hissed back. 'I've left all that behind. I'm Little Hawk now.'

'They won't mistake you for a solicitor's clerk,' Gully reassured him. 'But I'm not sure that being a Red Indian will help if we're caught trespassing.'

They had left the others camping in a wood a mile away, and had ridden the saddle-horses into the park. Tethering Betty and Brownie in a field behind a barn, they crept nearer the house on foot. Gully's teeth were chattering, partly with the cold and partly from fear. But Jerry seemed to be enjoying himself. They threw themselves down on their stomachs below the terrace wall.

'Now where?' asked Gully.

'Can't you do some of your *seeing*? Can't you work out where your friend is that way?'

Gully shut his eyes and concentrated, but nothing happened. Somehow he knew it wouldn't. The scrap of blue material didn't seem to work any more, and that worried him.

Jerry said, 'The daylight's fading. We might skulk around and try peeping in a few windows.'

Gully could just see the flash of his excited grin in the twilight.

They got up from their hiding place and crept along the front of the house, bobbing beneath the window-ledges so as not to be seen from within.

'Looks like a dining room,' Jerry whispered, peering round the edge of one window. 'Maid's setting the table. She can't see me.'

There was a shriek and a clatter of dropped cutlery.

'Oops,' Jerry said, ducking back down.

'We'd better lie low for a bit,' Gully hissed at him. 'Can't risk getting caught now. We don't even know if Clemency's here yet. Come on!'

And he scuttled off along the base of the wall, with Jerry right behind him. They threw themselves into the cover of a dense patch of ivy at the foot of a tower.

Gully coughed and spat. 'Ugh, cobwebs! Ivy's a filthy plant, always full of spiders.'

'Ssshhh,' Jerry warned him. 'Listen!'

They heard a step ring on the terrace, and a man's voice say, 'You're seeing things, Mary, there's not a soul out there. Too perishing cold, anyways. You girls, you let your imagination run away with you, and then you scream for help.'

Peeping round the wall, Gully saw a footman take another quick glance round the terrace and step back inside the front door. After he had closed it, however, another head poked out, a scared face with a maid's cap above it.

'Seeing things!' she muttered, and then, bolder, 'Ghosts or burglars—whatever you are—shoo!' And her head popped inside again.

There was a smoky scent in the night air. Gully said, 'What's that smell? It's getting stronger.'

'Just chimneys,' replied Little Hawk. 'No—look!'

To their amazement, a tiny raft of flames came floating down, spiralling to land in the shrubbery below the terrace. A hail of sparks like orange fireflies followed.

'What is it?'

'I don't know, can't make it out from here,' Gully whispered. 'But I'm going to have a look-see.'

He climbed out of the ivy and ran over the terrace, hurling himself into the bushes, which splintered and gave way under his weight. Jerry heard his muttered curses. He could just make out Gully's face, a pale circle, looking upwards to the top of the tower. Another shower of sparks drifted down. Gully waved at him to come over.

'Got a light? Anything to give a spark?'

'Yes, but what d'you—?'

'She's up there, signalling.'

'How can you be sure it's your friend?'

Gully tapped his forehead. 'I just do. But I don't know how she knows we're here, or even if she does. I've got to show her it's me.'

He grabbed the match-case out of Jerry's hand and began to strike the matches. The first successful one he held up near his face, then quickly blew it out. Jerry looked up too. At the top of the tower was a strange glow. As he watched, it became a brighter and he could see a figure leaning over the parapet and waving aloft a torch of flames. Bits of the torch broke away and came floating down, still alight. Then something dark, and fast, and a lot more solid than a floating flake of ash, hurtled out of the sky, just missing his head.

'Oh! Blast it, what in the name—!' he cried out, startled. Gully clamped one hand over his friend's mouth, and with the other groped around in the dark for the missile, whatever it was.

'Can't see,' Gully hissed. 'Let's get back under that window, there's enough light from indoors to see clearly there.'

The pair climbed back over the terrace wall and slithered to a safe place below the nearest lighted window. Gully handed Little Hawk a small paperweight carved like an owl, saying, 'That's what nearly crowned you. Good thing it didn't knock you out.'

While Jerry weighed the owl in his hand, Gully unfolded the sheet of paper that had been wrapped around it, and read:

Locked in the tower—found key to the top door, but not to the bottom one. CW.

P.S. I hid some getaway clothes in pineapple jar, hallway.
P.P.S. Trust no one.

While Gully was still pondering what to do next, Little Hawk reached out and picked up a shred or two of the blackened paper that had drifted down from the torch. *Great crested grebe*, he read on one fragment, and *Friday: rained all afternoo* on another.

Gully took one more look up at the tower. It was too tall to climb; he counted five storeys from the ground to the top. There was nothing for it but to venture inside the house. He signed to Little Hawk to follow him, and they found that the maid, in her fright, had left the great front door unfastened.

In the light from the camp fire, Fred was drawing red, black, and yellow stripes across Whitby's cheekbones. He paused, a stick of theatrical make-up in each hand, and said to Alf, 'What d'you think?'

Alf looked up and shrugged.

Fred completed the design with a single black stroke right down Whitby's sharp nose. Alf nodded in approval.

'It's like clowns,' Fred explained. 'They each have their own make-up. Somehow Josie's Red Indian make-up didn't suit Miss Whitby here. This 'un's much better.'

He handed a spattered bit of mirror to Whitby so that she could admire herself. She took a quick look, put the mirror aside, and stood up impatiently.

'Finished? Then I'm off.'

'Where?' Fred looked scandalized.

'I've had enough of hangin' around and freezin' my ears off. Gully with his psychic powers and Little Hawk knowing all about the place haven't come up with sweet tiddly-pom. I'm after that money what's owed us, and I'm not waiting any longer. I bet I can walk right in and find Miss Clemency Wrigglesworth as straight as I can spit!'

And with that Whitby pulled the zigzag-patterned Indian blanket tighter round herself and marched off into the dusk.

'At the very least I'll get myself warm!' she shouted back over her shoulder.

The lights of the Great Hall were ablaze in the distance. Unlike Gully, she strode in a direct line towards them, not bothering to hide. She wore her Red Indian costume over her own clothes for extra warmth, and her hair was still plaited Indian-style. The sky was fully dark by now and she was glad of the gleam of the snow to show her where to put her feet.

As she came up the slope towards the house she could see lights in numerous windows, casting a warm yellow glow on to the terrace. She expected to hear music and voices and laughter, to see elegant figures moving about the rooms. That was what went on in big houses: parties and dancing and tables groaning with fancy food. Clemency would be flouncing about in a silk dress, and would stick her chin in the air, pretending not to recognize Whitby. She'd tell that girl a thing or two—and her toffee-nosed relations!

But when Whitby reached the terrace she heard nothing. The rooms were lit but empty and quite still. She went along, as Gully and Little Hawk had done earlier, peering into windows, but she didn't creep and skulk. She came to the front door, marched up the steps and tried the iron handle. To her surprise it opened, and she found herself in an echoing hallway. The ceiling arched high above, a cave of shadows. A pair of curving staircases led up into the dark.

Whitby steeled her nerves. She bet that she had got further than those two useless boys, and she couldn't give up now, not having got so far. Nothing in the house stirred—except—she thought she heard a tiny noise, a light tapping and chipping? She paused outside a pair of double doors and listened.

Tapping and chipping. Whispering.

She slid one door open an inch and peeped through. But this was no way to make her presence felt. She pushed the doors wide and went in.

At the far end of a vast table sat a tiny woman dressed in ruby silk. She was cutting morsels off the food on her plate and taking bits on her fork and holding it beneath the table and whispering to whatever it was that was down there. She was so absorbed in this task that she still didn't notice when Whitby approached the table and spread her hands on its surface.

'I'm Whitby Marvel and I'm looking for—' Whitby began, in her loudest stage voice.

Before she could get any further, the tiny woman looked up, dropped her knife and fork, and screamed. Her plate went flying across the carpet, and a ripple of small furry creatures followed it eagerly. Whitby strode over to them: little, fussy, long-haired dogs. She picked up the smallest one and held it at arm's length. It had a cross, wrinkled-up face and bright black eyes that sparkled with fury. The woman stopped screaming at once and gasped, 'Please, no! I beg you not to harm Shu-Shu.'

'Shu-Shu, is it?' Whitby asked the dog, giving it a little shake. She felt a growl rumble through its ribcage.

The other dogs were at her feet. The largest had taken a corner of her zigzag blanket in its teeth and was backing away, pulling hard, while another was licking something delicious off her boot.

'Would I harm you?' Whitby asked Shu-Shu, who bared his teeth in reply.

Shu-Shu's mistress began to whimper.

'I'm not looking for a dog, I'm looking for a girl,' Whitby said to her sharply. Thank goodness she'd stopped screaming. Whitby couldn't stand screamers, and she had quite forgotten that her own appearance was rather unusual. And thank goodness that—so far— no great burly butler or footman had come to find out what all the noise was about.

'I'm Whitby Marvel and I'm looking for a little girl,' she began again. 'Thin, fair hair, big eyes. Looks like she wouldn't say boo to a goose.'

She put the dog down, and the little woman gave a sigh of relief. Shu-Shu instantly ran across the carpet and began whiskering up crumbs from around the fallen plate.

'There are no children here,' the woman said, beginning to recover her composure. She eyed the bell-pull that would summon the servants.

Seeing this, Whitby strode round the table and stationed herself between the woman and the chimney-piece where the bell-rope hung. Something weighed her down and dragged at her blanket. The fattest little dog was still clinging on with his teeth. She shook the corner of the blanket to try and throw him off. He growled and hung on.

'Ping-Ping!' his mistress said faintly.

'This is a most particular child,' Whitby insisted, muttering, 'Let go, Ping-Ping!' out of the side of her mouth and shaking the blanket again roughly. The dog swung from side to side, but hung on, with every appearance of enjoying himself. 'This child was sent for, to come to the Hall. Have you seen a child like what I've described?'

Miss Honoria Lestrange could answer honestly that she had not laid eyes on such a child. She expected Miss Clawe to dispose of the girl without disturbing *her* at all.

'There are no children here,' she repeated, 'only dogs.'

She could see now that this creature was no ghastly apparition like the ones last night. It was a human being dressed up in skins and beads and feathers, with a fierce expression painted on its face. But it was most worrying. That vision last night had warned about children. She trembled as she recalled it. And then this morning Miss Clawe had reported the girl missing. The house had been scoured, and men and dogs sent out into the park to search. Bow-legged Tam Jenkins and his stupid terriers couldn't find a rabbit unless it was under their noses! She couldn't help but make a triumphant snorting noise. *Those dogs* had no perseverance, not like her darling Ping-Ping.

Whitby heard the snort and it annoyed her. She noticed the woman's small hand sliding along the edge of the table. In a second she would reach out and yank on the bell-rope and all the servants in the house would rush in.

'Only dogs, eh?' Whitby repeated, swooping down on Ping-Ping and thrusting him firmly under her arm. 'Plenty of 'em, I see. So you won't miss this one, will you?'

And she was out of the room as fast as her legs could carry her, which, being a dancer, was pretty fast indeed.

Gully was *seeing* well. Whether it was the excitement, or the fear, or just the desperate situation, all his senses were strained to the peak of their powers. In the hall, faced with numerous vases and jars and pots, he went straight to the one with the pineapple lid. He was so confident that he let Jerry reach inside. Sure enough, out came a bundle of assorted clothes.

'She's got enough here to put on a three-act play,' Jerry said. 'What was she thinking of?'

'Thinking ahead,' said Gully. 'She's got a good brain, that kid. Sharp.'

'Like the things she throws,' Jerry remarked. He still had the owl paperweight, tucked into his Indian tunic.

'Come on. No time to lose. Got to find that tower.'

They leapt up the stairs, two at a time, until they were in the shadows above the hall. Gully put his finger to his lips, and they flattened themselves in an alcove as a maidservant came trotting along with a can of hot water. She paused with her back to them, seeming to listen out for something. Both boys held their breath.

The maid glanced fearfully a little way over her shoulder, as if not wanting to look too hard or too far. She shook her head and murmured to herself, 'Seeing things and hearing things! I'll be hearing about a new job and seeing myself into it as soon as ever I can.' And she hurried on down the corridor out of sight.

'It must be this way,' said Gully.

They entered Theodore's wing of the house. Gully followed his senses: Clemency was nearer now. He felt her presence like a buzzing in the top of his head.

'Down here.' He turned down the passage that led to the tower.

'Are you sure?' asked Jerry. They were in the heart of the house and escape would be very difficult if someone spotted them.

Right at the end Gully whispered, 'This door.'

Jerry tried it. 'Locked.' He bent down and put his eye to the keyhole.

'It's the right one, I know it. The door at the bottom of the tower. The one she said she hadn't a key to.' Gully's voice was low and urgent. He looked over his shoulder. The passage was dimly lit and empty. 'Now what do we do?'

'A spot of lock-breaking,' said Jerry, still bending down. 'Got any wire?'

Gully felt in the many pockets of his sagging jacket. String, penknife, an old spring, an apple core he'd saved for the horses, a forked twig that would make an excellent catapult . . .

'That'll do,' said Jerry, snatching the spring out of his hand and uncoiling it.

'Where did you pick up this particular skill?' Gully watched in admiration as Jerry bent the wire and twiddled it into the lock.

'As a law-abiding solicitor's clerk,' he replied. 'My father was always misplacing the keys to the office, or worse, the keys to the box where he keeps his money. We could break a pane in the office window, but there wasn't any way of getting into the box, short of picking the lock. An unscrupulous gentleman showed me how, and in return we waived his fee.'

'His fee for what?'

'Legal advice, of course. The judge gave him a year's hard labour, but I learnt this trick off him first. There, we're nearly done.'

'Someone's coming!'

They fell back into the shadows. The figure drew nearer, walking in a snappy, confident way. It was a short, broad man dressed in a thick overcoat. Gully could hear him whistling under his breath. In one hand he held a bunch of keys, in the other what looked like a large empty sack.

Chapter 25
The Little Hall

━━┼─○─┼━━

Down at the Little Hall, Molly Diamond was in a flap. She was quite unused to any bother these days. Her life looking after Sir Walter was as calm as a lily pond. Sir Walter was a man of great routine: he went nowhere and he did nothing. He took regular meals, and he slept a lot, with his old pet cat on his knee. He had no visitors and he lived such a quiet life that most of his neighbours assumed he was dead. Which suited Sir Walter and Molly down to the ground. The only people they ever saw were Tam Jenkins and Ermine the gardener.

So life went on for years until one wintry night, when, within a few minutes of each other, there came a great banging at the front door and a great rattling at the kitchen window, which sent Molly Diamond into a flap. Her cheeks flushed, her hair slipped from its pins, and her hands sweated so much that she had to keep wiping them on her apron.

She let the visitors in at the front door, for she recognized Mr Doggett, the solicitor, and she let Ermine and some little waif in at the back door and made them wait in the kitchen. She skipped into the parlour to wake Sir Walter, and stoke up the fire, and remove the supper tray. The cat stirred and yawned but Sir Walter went on sleeping. The visitors were entering without being invited through one door, and through another Ermine could be heard saying loudly that what he had to tell couldn't wait.

Molly stood in the middle of the floor, her hands full with the tray. 'Sir Walter!' she scolded. 'Wake up, if you please. Goodness knows what has happened!'

Mrs Potchard looked Poll squarely in the face and said, 'And you've seen Clemency not twenty-four hours ago and she was safe and well?'

'She was safe and well in the middle o' the night,' Poll said. 'We went on a raid.'

This hardly sounded like the Clemency she knew, but Mrs Potchard had to admit that the letter she held in her hand, the one addressed to Colonel Hibbert, fitted with the stories Clemency had told her of her life in India.

'And what did she look like?' Mrs Potchard asked gently, noting Poll's scared eyes and strained face.

Poll cast around for some description that would do: Clemency in her kitchen apron, or dressed in dustsheets with the candles held high above her head? 'Like that,' she said finally, pointing above the mantelpiece.

On the wall above the fire was a painting of a little girl holding a lamb by a length of blue ribbon. The girl wore a fussy old-fashioned dress and her hair was tied up in matching blue ribbon. It was a very fanciful and rather silly picture, thought Mrs Potchard, but all the same, there was a fair-haired, grey-eyed child not so very different from the Clemency she knew.

'She's right, you know,' Mr Ermine agreed, 'and Sir Walter'll tell you why.'

Mrs Potchard looked at Sir Walter, slumped in his chair beneath a tartan rug and a huge tortoiseshell cat. He seemed barely awake, but she saw the gleam of one eye and then he croaked, 'It's Lucie as a child. Lamb was the painter's idea. Dratted creature, wouldn't stay still. Puddle on the drawing room carpet, as I recall. And putting Lucie in ringlets! Scarecrow of a child— couldn't keep clean, *wouldn't* keep clean. Molly'll vouch for that.'

Molly stepped forward, blushing again.

'I was Miss Lucie's maid, you see, all through her childhood, right up till her . . .' She paused and coughed. 'Elopement.'

'Ran off, say it!' said Sir Walter. 'Ran off with a scoundrel! Broke your heart, didn't it, Molly Diamond? Admit it.'

Molly's eyes sparkled with tears.

'Wasn't only *my* heart as broke,' she said quietly. 'Never saw her again. But I should like to see her little girl, and if she's like that painting, then she's the image of her poor mother.'

'These pictures come from the big house, see,' said Ermine, anxious to get as much information over to Mrs Potchard as he could, having decided that she was the only sensible person present. 'Sir Walter had them all brung down here, Miss Lucie and her ma, all the pictures of 'em. They wouldn't give 'em house-room up at the Great Hall, anyways.'

'Molly Diamond!' Mrs Potchard said in wonderment. 'Then you were the one who wrote to Mrs Wrigglesworth—Miss Lucie—about her luggage and her missing umbrella? That letter was in the child's trunk. It's one of the clues that sent us here.'

'She kept it all those years? My letter! Oh, I do apologize for my terrible writing, ma'am. I blush to think that you seen it. Do you know, I never laid eyes on that umbrella again, can't think what could've happened to it.'

Mr Ermine coughed impatiently, and said, 'Well, what're we still waiting here for?'

'What do you suggest we do next?' Mrs Potchard turned to Mr Doggett, who grew pale. He had barely opened his mouth since arriving at the house.

'Suggest? Do?' he stammered.

'Storm the big 'ouse!' Mr Ermine cried, waving his fist.

Mrs Potchard was inclined to agree, but having got so far did not want to cause a catastrophe.

Ermine shouted, 'Demand that they bring out the little girl! Show us she's still safe and sound.' Puffed up to his full height he was barely more than five feet tall. Mrs Potchard could have wished for Gully, or better still, some burly constables.

'Come, Mr Doggett, we shall have to face them,' she said, in a firm voice. 'With your agreement, Sir Walter? Can Mr Doggett here say we speak in your name?'

'By all means, by all means,' Sir Walter rumbled. 'Give the scoundrels a good jolting. I'm all for a quiet life, but I'd be pleased if you'll see to it for me.'

'We'll take my Jem,' said Mr Ermine. 'He's a tower of strength.'

'And if you can spare me, sir?' Molly said. 'For I should like to go.'

Sir Walter, already drifting back into his snooze, waved a slack hand, and Molly ran off for her own hat and shawl.

As they were leaving, Poll tugged at Mrs Potchard's sleeve.

'There's somethin' else,' she said nervously. 'I didn't know what to make of it, but there was this boy—'

'Boy?' repeated Mrs Potchard.

'A bossy boy in a blue coat. He said the strangest thing . . .'

Something clicked at the back of her mind, and Mrs Potchard put her head close to Poll's to listen. When she had heard what Poll had to say, she looked even more worried. 'I wish we *had* brought the constables,' she said. 'Well, too late now. There's no time to lose.'

Gully went to follow Lysander into the tower, but Little Hawk grabbed him by the shoulder. 'There's only one door, and we don't want someone to lock *us* in. One of us has to keep guard.'

'But Clemency's up there—and *he* certainly looked a bad sort.'

'I know, but it won't help her if we get trapped too. Stay here.'

'Why me?' Gully protested.

In answer, Little Hawk raised one foot; on it he wore a soft buckskin boot, in contrast to Gully's heavy hobnailed ones. And peeping out of the top, Gully glimpsed a knife.

While Little Hawk disappeared inside the tower, Gully waited reluctantly, hardly able to hear a sound over the thumping of his own heart. All his senses were tuned to what was going on above him, but he couldn't make out anything except the buzz of fear.

Suddenly a door was flung open further down the passageway.

'Lysander? *Lysander!*'

Gully stepped back into the shadows. Too late.

'You there—come here! I've been ringing and ringing and nobody's answered. Whatever's going on?'

A small man in an embroidered dressing gown stood in the middle of the corridor, staring straight at him.

'Who are you? What are you doing outside my rooms? Are you one of Tam Jenkins' disreputable lot?'

Gully coughed and dragged off his cap. 'Housemaid thought she saw burglars. I'm just looking into it. *Sir*,' he added.

The small man clutched at his own embroidered lapels and glanced round fearfully. 'Burglars! Where?'

'Downstairs. But we've orders to check everywhere.'

'Good, good. I have a great many precious and important possessions up here, objects of great historical value. All my books and papers, too. Burglars would be glad to make off with those.'

'Yes, sir.' Gully clutched his cap and wrung it. He was desperate to get back to the tower door, desperate to know what was going on up there. But this old fellow wasn't finished yet.

'Downstairs, eh? Honoria will insist on using those great grand rooms, dining and sitting there all by herself.

Dancing the length of the ballroom, too, for all I know. Just her and her precious dogs. Let's hope if anything's taken it's something of hers. Perhaps they'll steal one of her dogs!'

And with that he went chuckling back inside his room and shut the door.

Clemency waited in Theodore's study, in the dull light of the fading fire. Gully was nearby, he was on her trail right now. But whether he could reach her was anyone's guess. She heard yet again the lock grinding as somebody opened the door at the foot of the stairs. The feet she could hear were familiar: Lysander's heavy tread. She looked for a hiding place, but there was nowhere in the small round room that could not be seen from the door. As Lysander flung it open, she dived under the desk. It made her feel even more frightened, crouching there just like a tiny mouse with a cat towering over it.

'No good hiding.'

A large hand reached down for her. Clemency scrambled away from it, to the far side of the desk, and climbed out again. She flattened herself against the bookshelves. Lysander threw a sack down on the desk. Looking broader than ever in his greatcoat, he pulled a small bottle from one pocket, a piece of cloth from the other.

'You can make this difficult if you like,' he said. 'No skin off my nose.'

'M-make w-what difficult?' Clemency stuttered.

Come on Gully, please, she prayed. Before it's all too late.

Lysander shook the little bottle over the wad of cloth.

'A scullery maid's gone missing,' he said, in a careless tone. 'Got caught stealing, and run off. The whole house is talking about it. Thing is, it's a terrible cold night to go running away. No surprise if they come across her body a day or two from now, frozen stiff, under some hedge. No surprise at all.'

Clemency shrank even further into Theodore's books.

'I won't cause any trouble. I'll . . . I'll . . . go away. You won't hear from me again.'

'That's not good enough for me. That's Miss Clawe's kind of thinking, that is. Slapdash. Weak. She thought you'd just fade away, down in the kitchen, a tender-brought-up scrap like you. Convenient, that. But not guaranteed. Well, I'm not taking any chances.'

'You can put me in the orphanage,' Clemency said, desperate. 'I *am* an orphan, anyway. I truly don't want anything more to do with my uncle and aunt. I promise I won't say a thing.'

Lysander shook his head slowly, with a look of grim determination. 'I've got plans, and you're not getting in the way. Not now, not ever again.'

He took a step towards her. Clemency moved one pace sideways, the only way she could go. Her hands slid along the shelves behind her, fingers spread out, clutching and clinging.

'I'll scream if you come nearer,' she said, trying a new tack. 'I'll scream the house down.'

Lysander smiled. 'Can't have you doing that, I'm afraid. That's why I brought this.' He raised his hand, bringing the pad of cloth nearer. 'I'm not a cruel man, see? I could've just hit you over the head.'

A flicker in the darkness behind him caught Clemency's eye. She took her attention off Lysander for a split-second. Out of the shadows leered a devil's face, striped and gleaming, glaring at her with terrible eyes.

Lysander, sensing her gaze shift, turned too, giving a quick glance over his shoulder.

'What the——?'

Her fingers slid over the windowsill, coming upon a cold brass tube. The devil made a roaring noise and leapt from the doorway. Clemency swung the tube and brought its wide end down on the back of Lysander's head.

He crashed over the desk, just like a felled tree.

'Good grief!' said the devil, crouching down. 'We'll give him a bit of his own medicine just to make sure.' And he pressed the wad of cloth over Lysander's nose and mouth. 'Ether. Knock-out drops. That should keep him quiet for a bit.'

He stood up. The two tall feathers of his headdress were battered and bent now, but Clemency recognized them from the park.

'What's that you hit him with?'

Clemency held it out with one trembling hand. 'Admiral Lord Nelson's very own telescope,' she said.

Chapter 26
The Taste of Danger

————||◦||————

Mr Ermine led the way with his lantern held aloft. Mrs Potchard followed, flanked by Poll on one side and white-haired Jem on the other. Molly kept stopping to help Mr Doggett pick his way, rather reluctantly, over the uneven path.

The lights of the Great Hall shone ahead.

Very many lights, Mr Ermine thought: something's up. 'We'll go in the front way,' he called back to his band of adventurers.

Mrs Potchard replied, 'We come in Sir Walter's name, *of course* we'll go in by the front door.'

Despite their numbers and the lights they carried, no one inside the house appeared to notice them as they marched over the terrace and up the steps to the great front door. Jem crashed on the iron knocker and

Mr Ermine bellowed, 'Open up, in the name of Sir Walter Lestrange!'

The door swung inwards of its own accord.

Mr Ermine muttered, 'Shouldn't wonder if they gets burgled, leaving it all open and inviting like that!'

Everyone trooped over the doorstep, glancing at each other in surprise and—almost—disappointment.

Inside, the house was very quiet. The little group stood in the entrance, looking about in wonder. It seemed deserted. But then some of them spotted a tiny figure, dressed in ruby silk, frozen at the foot of the left-hand staircase. She stared upwards with an expression of horror.

At the same moment, others noticed a tall, thin woman making her way in slow motion up the enormous staircase. She was dressed all in black and her hair was caught in a tight topknot. Keeping her back to the wall, her hands outstretched, she inched upward. Her eyes, too, were fixed on something high above.

A voice, clear and sharp, and familiar to Mrs Potchard, came from the darkness above.

'Tell me where she is, or I'll drop 'im. I know you've got her somewhere. I mean it, I'll drop 'im.'

'She *does* mean it, Clawe,' the tiny woman gasped. 'You should have seen her with darling Shu-Shu. She

303

shook him till his eyes nearly fell out.' She clasped her hands together and pleaded in a strangled whisper, 'Tell her, Clawe, tell her where the wretched girl is. Better still, fetch her here immediately.'

Miss Clawe looked at her mistress with a thunderous frown. Her topknot fell and rose again as her eyebrows worked. 'I'm afraid, Miss Lestrange, we have a *difficulty* there,' she whispered back, hoarsely.

'You heard!' the voice shouted from above. 'If you don't bring her out and hand her over to me, I'll drop 'im. Won't I?'

And something else up there in the shadows gave a half-swallowed bark.

Honoria whimpered. 'Ping-Ping. My poor angel.'

'Don't you remember what I told you earlier?' Miss Clawe hissed back at her. 'The problem in question is no longer *ours* to hand over. We shall have to try another way.'

Honoria huffed sulkily. 'Then it is *your* problem, Clawe. Just get on with it.'

The crowd in the hall looked on, open-mouthed, everyone—except Mrs Potchard—quite forgetting the errand on which they had come.

Miss Clawe paused in her climb and called out imperiously, 'Hand over the dog and then we'll hand over the girl.'

The voice in the darkness beyond laughed. 'I'm not that simple. Let's *see* the girl first, then we'll talk about what's to be done.'

Honoria was whispering again, quite unconscious of the crowd in the hall. 'Clawe, I implore you,' she said. 'Get the dog back. *Say* anything. *Do* anything.'

'I wouldn't do anything silly, if I was you,' the voice above said. 'I've only got to open my hands.'

Honoria sank on to the bottom stair like a collapsed umbrella. She groaned, 'Oh, my poor Ping-Ping. My poor pet.'

Out of the corner of her eye, Mrs Potchard saw a door open, a door with a green baize lining. She expected servants to come pouring through it, but instead a gangly figure in an ill-fitting brown suit slipped out, followed by a small person swamped by a tweed jacket and striped scarf. They disappeared into a bank of potted palms. Keeping an eye on the scene being played out upon the stairs, Mrs Potchard edged quietly towards the shadowy palms. That figure in brown had been unmistakable: her son, Gully. And up above, in the dark, was her niece Whitby. Whatever sort of fix had they got themselves into?

Miss Clawe went on speaking, and went on sliding herself up the staircase. With every word or two she

305

took another step. To those standing below she was almost in darkness, lit only from the lamps beneath her in the hall, a sepulchral, ghastly figure.

But now there was something—someone—else on the stairs. Mrs Potchard spotted another strange creature, moving in the shadows as cautiously as Miss Clawe had done, but making faster progress. He crouched low and his soft boots made no sound. He kept to the right-hand staircase while Miss Clawe climbed the left-hand one. No one else seemed to have noticed him. All eyes were on Miss Clawe.

'I've only to call the girl, and she'll come out,' she was saying. 'So hand over the dog. Just hand him over to me.'

There was no reply.

Miss Clawe lifted one sly foot and set it on the next step.

'Besides, you can't win now. What can you do? I let you have the girl, but you've got to get out of the house, and there are plenty of servants on hand to stop you getting away. So stop being a silly girl, and hand him over.'

The voice up in the darkness seemed to waver, then found its strength again. 'Your mistress doesn't seem to think I'm being silly. She wants her dear Ping-Ping back safe and sound. I want Clemency back safe and sound. That seems like a deal to me. She told you to do *anything* to get 'im back safe.'

'Yes, she did say *do anything*,' Miss Clawe echoed.

Now she was at the very top of the staircase.

Little Hawk, for that was who Mrs Potchard had spotted, was about twenty stairs below. He was now in a position to see as well as hear the person up there in the darkness. He could see the shape of her Red Indian outfit and her black plaits swaying forward as she hung over the banister rail with the dog suspended between her hands. He knew the voice belonged to Whitby Marvel, just as he had known from the very first moment he heard it below in the hall. Whitby hadn't seen him yet. She was too busy trying to keep hold of the plump, struggling dog. Nor had she seen how near Miss Clawe was getting, inching closer with every breath.

'And *do anything* is just what I have in mind!' Miss Clawe hissed.

As she said it, she lunged towards Whitby, not to grab Ping-Ping but to push Whitby over the banisters to the marble floor far below.

Gully had slipped out of the shelter of the potted palms and stood beside his mother. Both watched transfixed as Little Hawk touched the side of his boot and drew out something which caught the light and glinted. Gully was the only one of them who had seen him do this before. Gully was the only one who knew, or thought he knew, what was going on. It all happened in an instant. With perfect control Little Hawk threw the glinting thing. A sharp scream pierced the darkness.

Like a switch, the scream released the watching crowd into motion. Everyone spoke at once. 'What's happening?' 'Who was that?' 'What did he do?' 'Who screamed?' 'Who's been killed?'

They surged up the stairs, Gully in the lead, terrified of what he would find. The little woman in red silk—now far from collapsed—followed at his elbow, jostling him fiercely all the way. At the top he discovered Whitby clinging to a small dog. Little Hawk stood protectively beside her, ready to face the advancing crowd. And behind them, pinned to the wall, was Miss Clawe. Her eyes stared unseeing and her mouth hung open, but she was alive, simply rigid with shock. Little Hawk's hunting knife was driven neatly through her topknot.

Gully let out a laugh of relief. The woman in red pushed past him, flinging out her arms and crying, 'Ping-Ping, darling, come to me! I'll save you from that wicked creature!'

But ignoring his mistress completely, Ping-Ping snuggled up to Whitby and covered her face in adoring kisses.

'Perhaps someone should release that woman,' Mrs Potchard said, puffing her way to the top of the stairs, and nodding at Miss Clawe.

'Not yet,' said Little Hawk grimly.

Before anyone else could move to free her, a peevish white face, lit by a single candle, appeared from the gloom. 'What's all the noise? Have they caught the burglars?'

It was Theodore, stirring from his rooms for the first time in years. He stared round at the unfamiliar faces.

'I told that boy of Tam Jenkins', I've been ringing and ringing for an absolute age, and no one has come at all. It's absurd. Am I to be ignored in my own house? Just what is going on?'

'Indeed, brother, you may well ask,' Honoria said, her little face alight with fury. 'Kidnap and murder have taken place here tonight, and all you do is complain about the noise!'

'Murder?' asked Theodore, looking shaken. The candle in his hand wavered and almost went out. 'Who said anything about murder?'

'*She* was about to murder poor Ping-Ping,' cried Honoria, pointing at Whitby.

'And *she*,' Little Hawk shouted back, pointing at Miss Clawe, 'tried to murder this young lady!'

This was too much for Honoria, who sat down suddenly in a pool of red silk. 'Young devil, more like,' she muttered. 'I feel faint. Where are my smelling salts?'

But it was Miss Clawe who looked after the smelling salts, and Miss Clawe was not answering.

'We know that *kidnap* has taken place in this house,' said Mrs Potchard. She waved Clemency's note in the air. 'Here's the proof. And we have come with the blessing of Sir Walter Lestrange to remove the child unjustly held here.'

'What child?' Theodore began to bluster, but his sister just murmured, 'Take her, for goodness' sake, take her—if you can find her.'

'We'll summon the constabulary if you don't produce her immediately,' Mrs Potchard went on.

'Ma—' Gully began.

The odd little creature in tweed stepped out from between Mr Ermine and Jem, and began to unwind its long woollen scarf. 'I'm here,' she said. 'It's me.'

'Flea!' cried Poll, while Molly Diamond sighed, 'Miss Lucie to the life!'

Clemency felt herself pulled into Mrs Potchard's strong, warm arms. How could I have doubted her? she wondered. Or any of them—Gully, Poll, even Whitby? They were my loyal friends all along.

'Are you safe and well, child? No real harm done?'

'I feel safe now,' Clemency told her. 'As for harm . . .' She glanced at Little Hawk, but his face gave nothing away. From the safety of Mrs Potchard's motherly embrace, she said, 'Some of you believed I was a skivvy, and some of you . . .' making an evil face at her aunt, 'believed I was a wraith!'

Honoria clapped a hand to her mouth, but not before a small scream had escaped it.

'And both my uncle and my aunt thought I was a great inconvenience, to be got out of the way somehow or other . . . they really didn't care how.'

Molly Diamond spoke up. 'They wouldn't want your grandfather finding out about you.'

'My grandfather? He's still living?'

'He sent us to rescue you,' said Molly, which was almost the truth.

'So that's why they hid me, and locked me up! And Miss Clawe and Mr Lysander had their own plans for me, because I was an even greater nuisance to them. I stood between each of them and their hopes of a fortune. And a timid little girl could not be allowed to do that.'

Clemency felt Mrs Potchard's arms tighten around her as she spoke. 'I'm not sure about *timid*,' she murmured in Clemency's ear.

'Take her, we don't want her,' Honoria said faintly.

'Yes, yes, take her. We've had quite enough,' Theodore quickly agreed. Brother and sister looked at each other in horror to find that they were in accord.

'In the name of Sir Walter Lestrange,' came a quavering voice from the back of the crowd, 'and by the power invested by the law, I come to demand—'

Everyone turned to look at this last person to climb the stairs. He was interrupted by a cry from Little Hawk. 'Pa! What are you doing here?'

'Jerry, my boy . . .' Mr Doggett leaned weakly against the stuffed tiger. 'I feared it might be you when I saw that terrible knife. I had to look away.'

'It's all right, pa. I didn't hurt anyone. I never do hurt anyone.'

And to demonstrate this he walked over to Miss Clawe and pulled the knife out of the wall (and her hair). Miss Clawe slithered unconscious into a heap at his feet, which did nothing to reassure his father.

'No need for that, Mr Doggett,' Mrs Potchard said. 'The child is found. We'll leave this household—for now, at least—to sort itself out. Let's take Clemency to meet her grandfather. If he's awake,' she added, under her breath.

'You can't keep that dog, Whitby,' Gully said, as they all trooped down into the hall again.

'He doesn't want to go,' Whitby replied. 'I keep tryin' to put 'im down, and he jumps back up into my arms again. I don't even like dogs, 'orrible, snuffly, whiny little things!'

Honoria trailed after her, distraught, whimpering, 'Ping-Ping . . . come to me, darling Ping-Ping.'

'He must have liked the taste of danger you showed him,' said Little Hawk. 'His life's too dull in the ordinary way.'

'Then he's a bit like you before you became a Red Indian,' Whitby remarked. 'He'd better run away and join the circus.'

'Do you think they'll really summon the constables to investigate?' Little Hawk asked. 'There's been some dark deeds going on.'

Whitby shivered. 'I hope not. They might accuse me of dog-stealing.'

'They might accuse *me* of much worse. And as for Clemency—'

'What?' Gully and Whitby spoke together.

'You wouldn't believe what a little scrap like her could do.'

'I might believe it,' said Gully. 'She's got guts, that kid.'

Whitby nodded. 'I'll speak to Aunt Dolly. Persuade her it's best to leave things as they are.'

Little Hawk squeezed her shoulder fondly. 'You're a marvel.'

Outside in the cold dark air, Clemency and Poll and Molly Diamond and Mrs Potchard were walking in a row. They had a lot to talk about. But where the path grew narrow, they had to go in single file, and Clemency found herself behind Molly, who was leading the way with the lamp.

'There's the Little Hall where you grandfather lives, down ahead,' Molly said.

'I didn't know anything about a grandfather until today. To think, he was there all along—and so close!'

'He'll be that pleased to meet you. As I am.' Molly's voice was thick with love and pride. 'And we'll take such good care of you. But it's not nearly so grand down there as the big house.'

'Good,' said Clemency forcefully. 'I hated the big house. I'll be happy if I never set foot inside it again.'

As they all wound their way down the hill towards the lights of the Little Hall, Betty and Brownie, recognizing friends, let out whinnies of delight. And Gully remembered the apple core in his pocket, and fished it out, and broke it in half for them.

Afterword

Clemency Wrigglesworth went to live with her grand-father and Molly Diamond at the Little Hall, and if life there got too dull she would pop along to the kitchen gardens for a bit of entertainment.

Poll left the scullery and went to live with Mr and Mrs Ermine in the bothy. There Mrs Ermine taught her to read and write, and Mr Ermine taught her the gardener's trade. She discovered that she had a talent for it. Jem still did the digging and the simple tasks, but Poll found she could raise the most rare and tender of plants with her green fingers.

There were other changes at the Great Hall. The constables never were summoned. Miss Clawe retired, through ill-health, it was said, and went to live with a sister in the next county. Mary found a position with a jolly family in Bristol, and Nancy was promoted to head housemaid and soon to the post of housekeeper itself. Honoria, claiming to be weakened by shock, took to her bed and never got out of it again. Theodore, in perpetual fear of burglars, locked himself in his rooms and carried on his "great work". He now wrote his journals in a code which nobody knew but him. The family system of Curds and Clawes and Jenkinses broke down as the Great Hall got itself a reputation—for kidnap and murder and ghosts and devils—that put everyone off from working there. And Lysander and his relations were never seen again.

Mrs Potchard continued to ferry children around the world on endless journeys, clocking up more miles than all the other Potchards and Marvels put together.

As for what happened to Gully and Whitby and the Gen-u-ine Red Indians, that is another story.

About the Author

Julia Lee

Julia Lee has been making up stories for as long as she can remember. She wrote her first book aged five, mainly so that she could do all the illustrations with a brand-new four-colour pen, and her mum stitched the pages together on her sewing machine. As a child she was ill quite a bit, which meant she spent lots of time lying in bed and reading (bliss!).

Julia grew up in London, but moved to the seaside to study English at university, and has stayed there ever since. Her career has been a series of accidents, discovering lots of jobs she didn't want to do, because secretly she always wanted to be a writer.

Julia is married, has two sons, and lives in Sussex.

More
Oxford books
you might
enjoy . . .

—||—○—||—

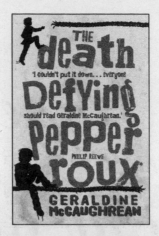

THE DEATH DEFYING PEPPER ROUX
Geraldine McCaughrean

On the morning of his fourteenth birthday,
Pepper had been awake for fully two minutes before
realizing it was the day he must die.

But Pepper isn't ready to die. So he sets sail on a sea of
adventures, inviting disaster and mayhem at every turn.

Join him on the run—if you can keep up . . .

'quirky and highly original'
DAILY MAIL

'irresistible reading'
SUNDAY TIMES

'A funny, charming and eccentric book'
OBSERVER

9780192756039

THE POSITIVELY LAST PERFORMANCE
Geraldine McCaughrean

The performances at The Royal Theatre are extraordinary.
You'd have to see them to believe them! But that's the
problem. Nobody can see them. Except Gracie, that is.

Newly arrived in her favourite seaside town and its beautiful
theatre, Gracie is quickly making friends. There's Mikey the Mod
who wears a parka and drives a scooter, Miss Melluish whose skirt
is missing, and Frank Stuart, the maker of mechanical elephants.

But the old theatre is under threat. Will Gracie and her
friends be able to save their home, or is the curtain set to fall
on their very last performance?

'Everybody should read Geraldine McCaughrean'
PHILIP REEVE

9780192733207

THE GREAT ELEPHANT CHASE
Gillian Cross

Tad and Cissie are on the run with Khush the elephant.
Clammy-fingered, steely-eyed Hannibal Jackson will
do anything to capture the animal.

Staying ahead means being faster and smarter—but
how do you hide an elephant? Especially one
with a mind of its own.

'An undoubted classic'
SUNDAY TIMES

'a rollicking good yarn'
GREAT BARR & ERDINGTON CHRONICLE

9780192789938

SKY HAWK
Gill Lewis

Something lives deep within the forest . . . something
that hasn't been seen on Callum's farm for
over a hundred years.

Callum and Iona make a promise to keep their
amazing discovery secret, but can they keep it
safe from harm?

The pact they make will change lives forever.

*'Opens your eyes, touches your
heart, and is so engaging it almost
turns the pages for you'*
MICHAEL MORPURGO

9780192756244

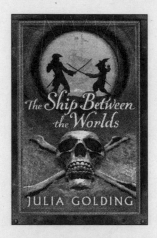

THE SHIP BETWEEN THE WORLDS
Julia Golding

When David Jones finds himself aboard a pirate ship, he knows
it must be a dream. Except that he's awake. And the 'dream'
is more like a nightmare.

David is swept up in the adventure of a lifetime: volunteered to
act as a spy on an enemy ship, marooned, and picked up by the
most fearsome band of buccaneers ever known.

Can he escape? The answer lies in the golden thread glistening
under the sea—and everybody is desperate to have it. Could it
lead David home, or to his missing father—or both?
Join him on the run—if you can keep up . . .

'high octane, high drama on the high seas'
LoveReading4Kids

9780192754837

RONIA, THE ROBBER'S DAUGHTER
Astrid Lindgren

High on the mountainside, a band of robbers live
in a great fortress.

Ronia, the daughter of the robber chieftain, roams the forests
but she must beware the grey dwarfs and wild harpies. When she
befriends Birk, the son of her father's greatest enemy, it causes
uproar. Ronia and Berk can no longer be friends—unless they
do something drastic. Like running away . . .

'[a] wonderful book, by one of the world's
best loved children's writers'
CAROUSEL

9780192789945